NORMAN  BONNIE

A LOVE STORY

WILLIAM GAILLARD ELLIS JR

authorHOUSE®

AuthorHouse™
1663 Liberty Drive
Bloomington, IN 47403
www.authorhouse.com
Phone: 833-262-8899

Published by AuthorHouse 07/01/2021

ISBN: 978-1-6655-3093-4 (sc)
ISBN: 978-1-6655-3099-6 (e)

Print information available on the last page.

One
C H A P T E R

*N*orman placed his coffee on the table beside him just before he leaned back in his lasyboy, adjusted the footrest just the way he liked it. Just high enough off the ground to reduce the pain in his knees. It was a cool morning and every time a new front came in his joints always ached. He reached for his coffee cup on the table beside him and took a drink. The bitter taste of the black coffee always relaxed him and while he was taking another sipped of the hot coffee, he noticed a humming bird feeding at the feeder hanging off the porch.

Norman watch it a second thinking "They will be going soon enough. It's the middle of September. This one must be a late traveler's and just getting a drink before continuing south. He must be for the Sun is barely up?"

It was early morning. A time he always woke upped

ever since he was a young man. He was now in his early eighties. His lower back was bothered him from sleeping in the same position most nights. It was mostly because his wife liked to have her back against his while sleeping. He tilted his head upward and could just hear Bonnie snoring lightly.

He thought how beautiful she always looked while sleeping. He shook his head and small tear came into his eyes as he reminded himself that she was slowly losing her mine. He smiled as he remembered all the fun they had when she was full of life. She always laughed at his silly jokes. Then all the loving she gave him at night in their bed.

"Gee, I miss that." Norman said.

He took another sipped of his coffee before he sat his cupped down and reached for his Guitar. Place it across his lapped. Then he plucked a G chord. Slowly he began to play one of his favorite songs:

"This World is not my home; I'm just a passing through."

"I've laid all my treasures just beyond the blue."

"The Angles beckons me from Heavens open door."
"And I can't feel at home in this world anymore."

He stopped playing and wiped another tear from his eye as he thought of his beautiful wife lying and dying in the other room. How often lately his eyes would fill with tears as she sat across the table and looked at him as if he was a stranger. Sometimes she would sit and stare out the window for hours not moving.

Often she would have asked, "Do I live here?" When they return home from going out to eat or when they return from Church which they loved to do since their younger days. There were times he would often rejoice when she would recall his name and remember as if she was normal. But, those times were getting farther and farther apart. Often there would be a day when she would not eat or even lose her way just going to the bathroom.

Their children would say, "Daddy, why don't you put her in a place where they could watch her closely."

Norman ignored their requests. He would tell them, "She was his wife and he swore he would take care of till she or he died and your Mother is not dead yet." The last sentence he always said loudly to indicate he did not like their request.

Suddenly the phone rang, which interrupted his wondering thoughts. He placed the guitar back against the wall beside the chair. Lowered the leg rest and walked over to the ringing phone. He didn't rush for he knew it was their youngest daughter, Clara. Who called everyday checking upon them?

When he picked upped the phone and said, "Hello."

Clara answered saying, "Daddy, just calling to see how Mother and you are?"

"Clara, "I'm find and your Mother still sleeping."

Norman replied. Clara said, "Well, you know she has a doctor appointment at two.

I'll pick you and Mom up at twelve thirty unless you want to go earlier and get something to eat?"

Norman said, "I think earlier be better. Let's say around eleven thirty. She will have a full stomach before seeing the doctor and you know she seems to do better when we do that."

"Ok," Clara returned. "Its six thirty now and will be eleven before you know it. Start her to get ready to go. I'll help if need be when I get there if that is alright with you?"

"It's alright with me." Norman answered. "I want to thank you for being a great help you know."

"Oh, Daddy, It's nothing really." Clara returned. "Besides, I really don't do much. You do all the cooking and cleaning. I just drive you and Mom around when needed and that is not very often. Oh, by the way, Freddy will be coming with us. School is out today and I'm so proud of him. He made the Honor roll."

"He did?" Norman said, "Well that is great."

"Anyway, I'll see you at eleven thirty." Clara said. "Ok," Norman answered.

Norman refilled his coffee cup before he returned back to his position in the lasyboy. As he sipped on his hot coffee, he noticed two hummingbirds fighting over the feeder.

"Strange," Norman thought. "One guards the feeder

till it takes a drink and leaves. Then another comes and guards it. They repeat that all day."

Norman glanced at the clock and it said, "Twenty till seven."

He could still faintly hear Bonnie's light snoring.

"She always snored." Norman thought. "I often would just lie beside her and listen. I do love her. Yea, I did save her life. I did are at lease she made me think I did. That was when I first met her." He let out a small laugh while said, "Then I made her my wife. Yea, that was back in 1948. I can still remember that day."

Norman leaned back into his lasyboy and began to dream and remember.

I remember it was one of those warn summer nights in July. I had just turned nineteen. I was still a kid back then. Just out of school and I loved to run at night around the community of Gafftop a small town along the coast of Texas where everybody knew each other. I knew all the streets an often at night would either run are walked them. As I traveled, the shadows and ghostly figures always gave me the sense of being in a foreign world. I was always thinking some monster would jump out at me from around some tree I was passing. But when I ran, I felt as if I was running at lease thirty miles per hour down the street. The bushes and trees seemed to just appear beside me in the darkness then were gone. It gave me the appearance of speed even though I was running not even ten miles per hour. I really loved to run. The cool summer night air seemed to invigorate me. I felt alive and I have not felt like that in years. The night noises, the dark houses, and the night full of stars were very addicted to me as I ran. They would call for me from my room when I first heard the Cicadas began to sing out their love song. I then would quietly leave the house while doing my best not to wake Mother or Dad. I would then either walk to the right are to the left. Sometimes the old Owl that live behind the house would hoot my leaving or a dove would flutter its wings from the dark oak tree in front of the house surprising me causing my heart to skip a beat. Back then I just loved to test my environment. To feel the strength of my body, testing it and I was always looking for a new adventure.

But the night I met Bonnie, I took a different path then what I usually take. I guess it was faith. For I usually stay away from the bayou because of the mosquitoes. They seem to just see me coming. But that night for some reason I decided to travel toward the bayou. That decision changed my whole life. Before then, I was just a young man who loved to fish and play different sports. For that night, I met the love of my life.

As I wondered slowly toward the bayou, I passed several of my friend's houses. You might say they were fishing buddies. We grew up together and our community was just a big playground for us. Anyway for some reason that night, as I left the house, I traveled the Bayou Route. The bridge crossed over to the east side of town. There the only small store in town, Brown's, was located that stayed open late. It was my designation. I think I was hungry are just wanted a soda.

Anyway, It was one of those really warn and muggy nights. Not a breath of wind was blowing and clouds hid the many stars above making the run really dark. In the stillness, I could hear my feet hitting the pavement as I ran. I was thinking of what I would get at the store when I entered the bridge. A mosquito was beginning to buzz around my head as I stopped running to walk across the bridge swatting at it and started to walk a little faster hoping it would go away. I moved over to the yellow line in the middle of the bridge. I had gone only a short way across the bridge, when I notice a girl in the dark whose leg was across the railing ahead of me and to the left.

I was thinking, she going to jump off the bridge. I sprinted toward her yelling, "Wait don't jump?"

My voice appeared to startle her as she slowly sank to the payment and my heart instantly went out toward her. When I arrived by her side, I was quit winded and my heart was racing from the short sprint. She was now sitting with her legs folded up against her. Her face buried in her hands. She was crying profoundly. I spoke not a word as I looked down at her. Those darn mosquitoes were still buzzing my around my head. Without thinking, I sat down beside her and wrapped my arms around her letting her pain and emotions flow into me. I felt her pain as if our souls were one and the same. I began to weep with her. Thinking what was so bad that she wanted to end her life here on this bridge. Of course, in the darkness she did not know the water was only about eight feet below the bridge and only four are five feet deep. It wouldn't have hurt her. It was just the concept of her actions that affected me. What made her take the first step onto the bridge? What if I had not made the decision to travel this way and had taken another route? She would have jumped and gotten hurt or even drown.

I spoke not a word as I held her close to me. Only the sound of the water flowing beneath the bridge from the incoming tide and the buzzed of mosquitoes broke the silence. I then noticed the time on her watch. It read eleven fifteen. I could not see her face which was buried in her hands. I did notice she had light blond hair which was tied back in a ponytail. It appeared to hang almost to the middle of her back.

She was wearing a nice blue top and a shirt long enough to cover her feet as she sat. At least in the dark her clothes looked blue. I realize I did not recognize her. In fact, I'd never seen her before and I knew all the girls in town and dated a few. But, just was not ready to settle down.

Several cars passed. None of them stopped to investigate why two people were sitting on the ground by the guard rail in the middle of the bridge. I did not move hoping her emotions would calm down. Her sobbing continued. I was hoping some reasoning was sinking into her being. That jumping off the bridge was not the answer to her problem. Suddenly, my feelings for this girl changed. I began to feel a love for her grow within my being as I held her. I began to notice the shape of her warm body lying against me and the smell of her hair that was flowing down across my chest. I never felt this kind of feeling toward anyone before. My thought went back to the times in my life I was rejected. Not wanting to live. It was always just a passing thought and one which I rejected immediately. Taken a life, even one's own life is just way beyond my concept. Why she tried to jump was reviving through my mine. Such a pretty girl and she has so much to look forward in life.

Every now and again she would shiver and tighten her hands on her face. It appeared as if some great relief was beginning to entering her being. As if my holding her, helped her to overcome the reason for her emotional stress. I glanced at her watch. It read eleven twenty-five. Another car passed exposing us for a second. Then, there on the ground I notice a card. I could just make out the inscription in the dark. It read, "My Dear Darning Daughter."

The words made me wonder if this card was the reason for her being on the bridge. Curiosity was growing in me to reach for the card and read it. But, I didn't want to change my position beside her with my arms around her until her emotions settle down.

I was pondering over the card when the next car that

appeared came to a screeching stopped beside us. The car door opened and a large man appeared very disturbed and yelled, "What are you doing with my daughter?"

As he then came toward us to separate us, I said, "Holding her. I think she tried to jump into the bayou from the bridge." My words stopped him cold. He began to see me as a savior instead of some guy out to hurt his daughter.

"Daddy," spoke a small meek voice from the girl in my arms. "Oh, Daddy, I'm so sorry." she said just before she began to cry again.

Her Daddy sat down beside her. I released her which aloud her Dad to take my place. As I stood, my legs hurt from being beside her without moving for what must have been an hour. As I stood, I picked the card up I had notice on pavement and placed it in my back pocket.

"Oh, Daddy," her meek voice said again as her Dad placed his arms around her.

"There, There, Bonnie, everything is going to be alright." He answered. "It was just her time. I know you loved her and were very old world."

"You really think so, Daddy?" She asked.

"I do." He answered. "She wouldn't like it if you were to do something foolish, now. You have a full life ahead of you. I believed she would like to see some grandchildren first. I can see her telling God how good a daughter you are and asking him to take care of you. I just know he loves you as I love you and I know he wants you to have a long and beautiful life."

"Oh, Daddy, I'm so terribly sorry to make you worry over me." Beth answered before she looked upped at me. I could just make out her tear stained face in the dark and Right off, I could see she was a beautiful young lady my age.

Still looking at me she said, "I was not going to jump off this old bridge. We buried my Mother today and I was so upset I went for a walked. When I entered the bridged I caught a cramp in my calf and was just stretching it out the railing when you saw me."

She looked at her Dad and said, "You believe me. Don't you, Daddy?"

He answered, "I believed you. I surly do."

"Son, what is your name?" Her father asked me.

"Norman," I answered. "Norman Toms."

He reached out his hand toward me and said, "If you will help us to our feet. I will take Bonnie home."

I helped him to his feet. Then both of us helped Bonnie to hers.

Then he helped her into his car after I quickly went before them and opened the door. Her emotions seem to have calmed down as she settled into the car seat. The present of Father was very comforting to her. I could see right off that he loved her dearly.

After he closed her car door, he turned to me and held

out his hand which I shook. Suddenly, Bonnie emerged from the car and wrapped her arms around me. Squeeze me a second before she reentered the car. She looked at me and the most wonderful smiled filled her face.

Her Father paid little attention to her movements as he reached into his wallet and handed me a card. As I took the card he said, "Call me anytime, Norman. I think you are just the young man I'm looking for."

He then closed her door again. Walked around and entered the driver seat. Then he drove away leaving me alone on the bridge. At the end of the bridge he turned the car around. As they passed by me, both Bonnie and her Dad waved at me. I watched them till they were out of sight before I looked at the card her Dad had given me.

It read, "Wayne Sisk Auto Repair, Sales and Service, Call Ca4-6758 between 8-5 Mom-Sat.

I placed the card in my wallet. Pulled out Bonnie's card and looked at it for a second before replacing it back into my back pocket. I decided right then and there I would not read it or even give it back. The card was way too dangerous for Bonnie to have back. To read it I would be entering a private affair which was none of my business. If I gave it back to her, she could again become so sad she just might return back to the bridge and finish what she was going to do tonight. Of course she said she was only out for a walk. But, if I give it back tomorrow she could say, "I stole it."

That lone mosquito or another was still bugging me as I continued toward Brown's. I stopped as a thought ran through me I should throw the darn card into the Bayou. "Darn it." I thought. "I'll keep it and later after she feels better give it back to her. That want do either."

I continued walking and as I near the end of the bridge, I made my decision. "I think it is best I keep it hidden. For I know one thing, I'm going marry her. If I give it back it will make a mess of our future relationship. Yep, I'll hide the card and after we have been married, let us say twenty-five years, and then I'll give it back."

My steps became lighter as I left the bridge behind. I had made my decision concerning the card and my heart was beaming with joy. Even the mosquito wasn't bothering me anymore. I picked upped my pace towards the convenience store. I knew it was getting late. I had nothing to do tomorrow anyway. Mom and Dad never fussed on me for my late night excursions. Thou sometimes, Dad would voice a concern when I slept all morning.

They were also concerned about me being drafted because of the Korean War. I told them nothing I can do about it. If I'm drafted, I'm drafted. Still I was fairly free specially sense I just graduated from High School. I was thinking about these things as I headed for the store. My mine continued to wonder back to Bonnie. She got me thinking about my future which until now I was leaving to chance.

I was almost at the store when a car pulled up beside and rolled down its window. It was Officer Danny Treat. He said, "Hello, Norman."

"Hi. Danny." I said as I stopped and turned toward his car.

"I see you are out on one of your excursions?" Danny asked.

I just smiled and said, "Well, I could be or maybe I could not. I'm not answering. But, I will tell you one thing. I'm going to marry a girl I met tonight on the bridge. She the most beautiful and wonderful girl I have ever met. Her name is Bonnie Sisk. I just know. You know what a mean.

"That's good." Danny said. Well anyway, I hope after you marry her you have twenty kids." Then he laughed and said, "Got to go. See you around."

I could hear him laughing as he drove away. Soon, the only sound I heard was the tapping of my shoes hitting the pavement as I walked. As I began to enter the tree area before the store I could hear cicadas calling all around me. As I walked the small hill leading upped to Brown's, I noticed the sound the cicadas made as I walked. Their song seemed to changed pitch as I passed. Either their sound pitched went from high to low are low to high. It appeared it appeared as if it was a directional single. "Yea," I thought, God sure knows how to make creatures. Those cicadas can send out sound waves out as if it was a directional finder. If it is high, then their future mate was going in the wrong direction. They must travel down the low pitch line. Of course, it could be other way and have to travel the high pitched line. Either way I guess."

As I entered Brown's store I was greeted with, "Norman, I have not seen you in a coon's age. How you been boy?"

"Just fine, Mr. Parkman." I answered.

"You're upped pretty late aren't you? It is almost midnight." Mr.

Parkman asked before turning the radio down to hear me better.

I did not answer him as I opened the cooler and grabbed myself a cold coke. Popped the lid and took a drink. It felt good going down.

"I can see you are pretty thirsty also." Mr. Parkman said as he stood to stand over the cash register.

"That I am, Mr. Parkman. I've been dodging mosquitoes all the way here." I said just before I took another drink. "You know I like to run at night, Mr. Parkman. I've been busy doing odd jobs all summer and just hadn't the time lately to do much running. Tonight, I thought I would just run over here and get myself a soda."

"Glad you stop by," Mr. Parkman returned. "It has been real slow tonight and at times I thought about going home and quitting this job. I'm going on seventy now and been thinking I'm too old to work. Still I need the money. Like you, got have some spending money to blow on the girls." He laughed.

"We do at that, Mr. Parkman," I answered just before I laughed with him. "But, I met a girl tonight I'm going to marry. The prettiest girl I've ever seen. She had the prettiest long blond hair, blue eyes and a body to go with it."

"You did? What's her name?" Mr. Parkman asked.

"Bonnie," I answered. "Bonnie Sisk."

"Oh, I know her." Mr. Parkman said, "She the daughter of the new owner of what use to be Fred's Auto Repair just pass Calvary Baptist Church out on highway 46. Heard he was looking to hire. Thinking of working for him?"

"Maybe, He offered me a job tonight I think." I replied. "Anyway I got to go. Here the nickel for the coke and thanks."

"Come back and see me more often. Will you?" I heard Mr. Parkman say as I went out the door.

Humming cicadas greeted me as I entered the dark. I walked sometimes trotted my way back home. My mind wondering on what I should do. How was I going to date Bonnie? I thought, "I'll just go upped to her and introduced myself and say, Hi, I'm the guy you met on the bridge, remember. No, that not the way. I'll just get a job working for her old man. I'm bound to meet her then. I then could introduce myself to her. Wonder if she would shake hands or even hug a grease monkey. Is she even out of school yet? Maybe she only fifteen and not eighteen I think she is." I struggled with these thoughts all the way to the house.

My Mother always worries about me leaving the house

in the middle of the night. So as I entered our yard, I notice the porch light was on. She does that every time, I leave. Then she fusses on me for sleeping till noon. As I entered the house, I turned off the light. Making sure I make as little noise as possible, I stopped and got a good cold drink from the fridge, grabbed myself two donuts, and headed for my bedroom. Still trying my best to make as little noise as possible, I entered my bedroom when a thought hit me as I pulled Bonnie's card from my back pocket. "I hope I do not have to defend myself to much tomorrow over helping Miss. Bonnie."

As I sat down upon my bed, I reach under it and pulled out my keepsake box. The boxed was unlocked with the key safely inside. That way won't lose it was my theory. I opened it and noticed the few keepsakes I kept in it. My favorite marble, my first babies tooth and a ticket stub from going to see the country fair. I laugh to myself as I looked at the few things I've kept. I was going keep everything I did to remember later what I did.

"Oh Well, at least I still have the box." I thought as I placed Bonnie's card into it. Closed the lid and replaced it back underneath my bed. As I undress, I thought, "I'll never read that card. Way too personal and way too dangerous to give back. Maybe it would best I threw it away. If she asked about it, I'll plea dumb and tell her it must have fell into the bayou." I was still thinking of her as I drifted off to sleep. What a night it has been. What a night.

Two
C H A P T E R

*N*orman pulled the small Lock Box from among the other keep sakes in the closet, its hiding place after selling the Auto Repaired business close to twenty years earlier where he kept it well hidden to keep Bonnie's prying eyes out of it. The key still rattled in it as he carried it back to the living room and regain his position on the lazyboy. He positions the box on his lapped and slowly opened it. He had added nothing to the box after placing Bonnie's card in it many years ago. Always afraid to open it less he could not resist reading the card.

"I've kept this from her all these years." Norman thought. "I wonder if she would read it now without becoming too emotional or real mad at him for keeping this from her. I wonder if it would jar her memory back." Norman looked at the card for several minutes afraid to touch it. The message still read, "My Dear Darling Daughter." With trebling hands Norman slowly removed the card and holding it up to the lamp light brought back the same spiritual feeling he had for her as he held her on the bridge so many years ago. Norman brought the card back to the lock box opening while feeling the smoothness of its surface. Then with trebling hands, he replaced it back into the box and closed the lid hearing it click into place. Norman took a deep breath as a sign of relief filled his being. Norman fingered the lock box and thought, "Bonnie asked about the note the next day. Oh yea, that was when Tom Sneed and his gang met her."

Norman laughed as he lean back in the lounge chair placing the lock box upon the table beside him and began to remember saying, "Yea, I remember sleeping till Mom woke me around eleven thirty yelling, "Get up Norman. I've got you some lunch ready. Your Dad wants you to go and catch him some bait for tonight. Uncle John coming over and they are going fishing tonight. He said he would not have time to catch some after he gets off work. So get up now."

I rolled out of bed, took a shower, got dress and headed for the kitchen. Mom was reading some love novel at the kitchen table as I entered. Mom's kitchen that was all white. White walls, white floor, white counter tops, white cabinets and Mom were even sitting at a white kitchen table. Behind her were also two white windows with white drapes located on each side. Mom looked upped at me as I entered and she said, "Made you two sandwiches and placed them in the fridge."

She looked quit motherly with the only light in the kitchen coming through the windows behind her. A light Gulf breeze was fluttering the drapes. It gave her a glowing appearance. I stood looking at the picture before me a second before continuing into the kitchen.

Mom sat the novel on the table and repeated, "Your Dad and Uncle John are going night fishing. He told me to tell you when you woke upped to catch them some bait and leave the bait bucket beside the boat."

"Sure Mom." I answered as I walked to the fridge and retrieved the sandwiches she had made for me. As I sat down at the table, I said, "I'll try to catch some. At lease I'll try."

"Did you have a good run last night?" Mom asked looking at me over her glasses. "There has been a rumor of a girl being helped by a young man last night at the bridge. That would not be you, would it?"

I smile at her as I took a good bite of my sandwich. She waited.

Looking at me with that look she had when she already knew the answer and just wanted me to put my foot in my mouth.

Mon said, "I'm waiting."

"Mom, you said it was just a rumor." I said as I took another bite of my sandwich.

"Norman," Mom said still looking at me over her glasses. "You know I already know all about it. I'm just waiting to hear your version. Are you going to tell me are do I have to drag it out of you?"

I set my sandwich down and said, "Mom, it is no big deal. While running last night, I decided to run over to Brown's. While crossing the bridge I notice a girl that look like she was going to jump into the bayou. I yelled at her and she collapsed. I went to her side and held her for she appeared to be in some kind emotional stress. Her Father showed upped and I found out her Mother had died yesterday and she was just grieving. All I did was hold her and quickly learned she was not going too jumped. She said she had a cramp in her calf and was only trying to message it out when I saw her with her leg on the railing."

I picked upped my sandwich and said, "Is that enough information for you?"

"Well, if that is all," Mom said as she took a drink of her tea, "I guess this money and the Thankyou note that came with it you will not need." Mom smiled as she reached into the pocket of her apron and pull out a note written on light blue paper along with several fives and placed it on the table in front of me, leaned backed in her chair and waited watching me closely. She had a smile upon her face and her eyes kind of twinkled.

I took another bite of my sandwich and eyed the note. I set my sandwich down. As I reached for the note I said, "Well, maybe I did a little more than just hold her last night. But, giving me a reward for doing something for my future wife is something I would done a thousand times."

"Your future wife, you say?" Mom said, "Hmmmm"

I counted the fives which added upped to fifty dollars. Placed them on the table and began reading the note out loud. It read,

"Norman, I want to sincerely Thank you for being there for my daughter when she was at her lowest over her Mother's death. As a token of my appreciation and thanks, I've given you fifty dollars to do with as you please. I know right now you are thinking I do not deserve this reward. Let me say to you, it is my way of showing you that I love my daughter dearly. If it had not for you, she might have hurt herself. In my eyes you deserved many times the fifty. I also want to remind you that I am hiring and would like to hire you to work in my new garage. I will train you and give you a future. Truly Thank you, Wayne Sisk."

I read the note one more time. Then I looked at Mom who was smiling and still looking at me over her glasses. I placed the note backed on the table, picked my sandwich back up and took another bite avoiding eye contact with her.

"Are you going to tell me what happen are not?" Mom asked.

I said, "I already told you, Mom. I saw her at the edge of the bridge when I was running last night. I thought she was going to jump into the bayou. I yelled at her. She collapsed upon the payment. I ran to her, and then I held her for she seemed to be in such a stressful state of mine. As I held her, I fell in love with her. So I have decided I'm going to win her heart and marry her. She's very beautiful and her name is Bonnie."

I smiled at Mom as I finish my first sandwich and took a drink of my soda. Then I said, "Is that enough for you, Mother. Now you can spread it all over town."

Mom still had a big smile on her face as she said, "If that is all you did, then I'll be good not ruin your life by spreading your story all over town. Besides it would insult this girl you are going to marry. You know how a rumor can spread and turn into a lie. I'll just let you put your own foot into your mouth and it will be a good one I bet." She continued to smile as she left the table to refill her tea glass.

As Mom walked back to her seat she said, "I would love to meet her one day. I think Dad would also. Especially sense you're going marry her."

"I am going to marry her, you just wait and see." I answered back as I took another bit of my sandwich.

She just looked at me with a sparkle in her eye as she watched me finish my other sandwich. I finish my soda, excused myself and headed out the back door. Mom watched me leave before returning back to her Novel.

Their house was built about eight feet off the ground near the edge of Gafftop Bayou where the town got its name. Dad built a nice deck, steps and pier around the house and along the edge of the bank. Dad's rowboat was docked next to the pier and ready for fishing trip with their rods and tackle already in the boat. Almost every weekend, Uncle John and Dad would often row down the Bayou to their favorite fishing spots along the Bayou, fish and crabbed till after dark. Bring their catch home and have a fish fry and crabbed boil. They always caught enough for us and the neighbors.

I went around the house to the storage building and located the casting net. Grabbed a bucket and headed for what I have found to be the best casing spot to catch some mullet near the house. Within a few casts, I had gathered a bucket full of shrimp and mullets. That will do them, I thought as I returned to the boat. I pour the bait into their bait bucket and hung it over the side of the pier beside the rowboat. I then wash the casting net and bucket and hung the net in the storage building.

I returned to the kitchen, grabbed another soda, the fifty bucks off the table and headed out saying, "I'm going to check out this job offer. I should return home by supper."

She looked at me from her novel and said, "Don't spend that fifty on junk food, now. We will be having fried fish and crab cakes for supper. Remember Aunt Eva and Uncle John is coming over."

"Ok Mom." I said as I left forgetting and let the screen door slam shut a, "Norman, shut that screen door like you are supposed to," followed me as I exited onto the pouch.

"Sorry Mom." I yelled back as I headed down the stairs toward the gravel street that ran in front of the house.

I traveled the three blocks to Highway 46. As I rounded the corner, there in front of Grace's Hamburger and Malts, Tom Sneed gang was talking to Bonnie. She was laughing at something Tom had said. She looked all the more radiant with a white blouse and a red dress that hung just passes her knees. Her blond hair was pulled back in a pony tail and held there by a sparkly hair broach. I almost rushed to her defense but thought better not. She might be defended by claiming her as my girl friend just yet. I slowly walked toward them and heard Tom say, "So you are new in town? Where you from if I may ask?"

"Alvin," She answered.

"I've been there. Nice town. So why move to this small town here on the coast of Texas?" Tom asked just as he reached and took hold of her arm and started to lead her inside the Diner.

"My Dad opened an auto repair place here is why." She answered as she pulled her arm away from him. "And I don't want to enter the diner. I'm going to the bridge that crosses the bayou and look for something I dropped."

Tom stepped away from her and said, "I'm sorry, I

thought you were going inside. I'm Tom Sneed and this guy here my brother, Jeff and his friend Billy beside him."

Tom then pulled out a comb and quickly combed his hair that had gotten out of place when Bonnie removed her arm from his grasped. He wore it with a flattop and duck tails on the side. Many of the local girls had a crush on him and he played the part quit well.

Bonnie said, "Well, I'll see you around. I got to go."

She started to leave when Jeff asked her, "Can we come with you and help you look for your lost item?" Jeff was the youngest boy in the Sneed family. He was trying to copy his older brother's dress and hair style. The other boy was Billy Treat, son of Deputy Danny Treat. His father kept his hair cut short. He seems to like it that way, anyway.

As Bonnie was turning away from them, she saw me and stopped and a smile came onto her face for a second, but change when I stopped before her saying, "Hello Bonnie, You seem a lot chipper today. I see you have met the Sneed brothers and Billy."

Bonnie expression was more serious when she said, "I was hoping I would fine you. I dropped something very precious on the bridge last night. I am wondering if you might have seen it." It was a card from my Mother. I was so upset and did not notice I had lost it till I was home. Maybe you saw it before you left the bridge?"

"Nope," I lied. "We can go look for it if you like."

Suddenly behind her Tom spoke upped and said, "I'll

drive you to the bridge and helped you look for this card you lost. That way you won't have to walk there." Tom then pointed to the black Dodge pickup parked by the diner and said. "It is a lot better riding then walking. Don't you think?"

My heart sank as she said, "Sure that would be a great help. My legs are tired and I would just love to ride in your truck, Tom."

I started to say something but thought otherwise when Tom held out his hand and Bonnie took it. I watched as he opened his passenger truck door allowing Bonnie to climb in. Cross to the other side, entered and start the truck motor. The other two climbed in back. As he backed out, my mind was racing should I go with them are not. But, before I could react, Tom gunned the motor and they were gone.

I watched them till they were out of sight. Then I headed toward Wayne's Garage. As I travel I thought, "That darn Tom Sneed anyway. He always steals my girl friends. But I think Bonnie smarter then he thinks and is not fool by his charm."

I was really feeling down as I walked into the garage. I was mopping over what had happen at the diner. Mr. Sisk was stuck under the hood of a black Chevy pickup just talking to his self. "Come on out you booger. Gee, I hate these bolts that get stuck and hard to reach. Darn it." He sign with relief as a bolt dropped to the floor below.

When he came out from under the hood, he saw me.

"Hello, Norman. I was hoping you would show up today." Mr. Sisk said as he wiped his hands on a rag.

"Mr. Sisk, I've never worked on a car before." I said as I walked around and looked under the hood of the truck examining its engine. "Are you sure you want me to work for you? I know nothing about cars at all."

Mr. Sisk stopped wiping his hands with the red rag before saying, "Norman, I wasn't looking for someone that knew it all. I was looking for someone I could train and work my way. Then when I leave them with a job, I know it would be done right."

I looked back under the hood at the motor thinking for a second before I reached out my hand and said, "Well, I guess I'm your man." "Good," Mr. Sisk said as he took my hand and we shook. We both laugh.

As he released my hand, he continued, "It will be fun. You'll see. It also will give you a future as well as a source of living. The world is changing fast. This war has brought out the best in America and technology is moving faster pace then there are technicians to keep it operating. You see, we are the technicians that keep the cars on the road. Make money as we work doing it. Otherwise, there would be broken down cars everywhere."

He then walked toward the front of the garage. I followed. He then pointed toward the two cars parked outside. "See those two cars and unless we fixed them, they are nothing but scrap. That is where we come in. We will bring one car at a time into the shop and fix it. The owner then can drive their lovely wives around again. I will show you what needs to be done. Then in the future you will know what to do without me telling you. Because by teaching you to do it correctly, I then will trust you to do the work by yourself without me standing over your shoulder are even being in the shop."

Mr. Sisk patted me on the back as we reentered the garage and went into his office still wiping his hands with the red rag. He walked around his desk, sat down and said, "Have a seat Norman."

He opened one of the desk drawers, removed several forms and placed them before me. "Fill these out for my records. I'll be outside working on that Chevy pickup. Just fill out what you can and leave what you can't blank. Just leave them on my desk when your finish."

The forms were mostly blank when I got done because most of the questions had nothing to do with me. I sign them and left them on the desk. When I reentered the garage, Mr. Sisk was working on a generator at the work bench. I watched him replace the bushing and brushes. He looked at me several times explaining the working of the generator and the problems that occurred with them. When he had finish and started to return to the pickup I asked, "Mr. Sisk, you didn't tell me how much I'll be making?"

"Do you think I should pay you full pay while in training?" he answered.

I thought a second while rubbing my chin then said, "I guess not." As he began to reinstall the generator, Mr. Sisk said, "I thought you would say that, Norman. What I'm going pay you in the beginning does not reflect what you will receive later. How about two dollars a day to start with? Then after you have learned a few things and become more confident in yourself in solving what is wrong with a car and able to fix the problem. I then will increase your pay to what is normal for good mechanics. You must understand that motors are not the only problems your face. There also transmission problems, front end problems and rear end problems. You will learn the different tools we use. You're also learned to use the blow torch and welding unit. Your learned the different types of oil used as well as doing body work on dented finders. There is so much to learn that even I after all the years working in this business still learning."

"Sounds good to me?" I said, "When do I start."

"Monday," Mr. Sisk said as placed another mounting bolt in place. "See you then, Mr. Sisk." I said as I left him under the hood of the pickup.

I had gone just a few feet out the garage when Tom's trunk pulled into the drive followed by the dust from the gravel road. Bonnie was now riding in back with Jeff and Billy. They were laughing and seem to be enjoying themselves. Her hair was windblown. I could also see a bit of hay stuck to her blouse and skirt as she stood. Tom raced the motor couple times before killing it. He was smiling as climbed out of the truck and walked toward the rear. Jeff and Billy climbed over the tail gate onto the ground. Billy lowered the tail gate. Then as Bonnie walked to the rear, Tom held out his hand to help her which she promptly refused saying, "Tom, I got up here by myself. I can get down myself."

Still holding out his hand Tom replied, "Now miss. Bonnie, I would hate for you to hurt yourself as you climb down. Just take my hand and I'll help you. I would not want your pretty clothes to get anymore dirtier than they already are."

"Now that you put it that way, I guess I will let you help me." Bonnie answered just before she jumped to the ground while grabbing Tom's hand as she went. It did little to stop her from taken a couple steps forward as she landed knocking into Billy. Whom, She then pushed into Jeff. Tom did his best to stop her forward momentum but it was no use. She continued forward tripping on Billy's extended leg sending her and Tom spilling toward the ground. Her laughter rolled as she hit the ground. Tom was doing his best not to land on top of her. While Billy, at this time was still trying to stay up, he tried to grabbed hold of Jeff's arm. But, he was laughing too hard and missed it and ended up on the ground also. Their laughter just rolled which I joined in. It was quite funny.

Tom, lying on his back said, "I do not think that was quit the way I planned for dropping you off at your Dad's shop."

Bonnie, quickly picked herself from off the ground and shook the dust off her skirt. Smile at Tom on the ground, glanced over at me and smiled with one of those little smiles a girl does when she very pleased with the outcome of her actions. Then quickly ran into the garage just a giggling.

I watched her leave before helping Tom off the ground.

"She something else isn't she? I said to no one in peculiar.

"I think her nuts." Billy said, as he picked himself off the ground. "I like her." Tom said as he dusted the dirt off him. "I think she is different in a way. She is really fun to be with. Never know what she is going to do."

Tom then turned to the two boys and said, "Get in the truck. We got to go fetch Mom at the store. She should be finish by now and should be waiting for us."

Jeff and Billy quickly climbed back into the bed of the truck. Tom reentered the cab. Looked at me for a second and gave me a smile before he started the motor. Back out into the street. Then gun it as he headed back into town.

As I watched them leave, I thought of reentering the garage and introduced myself to Bonnie. There was a dance this Saturday at the

Top Fin Bar and the fifty was burning a hole in my

pocket. I was pondering over to enter or not when from the garage door Bonnie said, "I thought they would never leave."

Bonnie slowly walked outside looking at me with her head going back and forth studying me. She placed her hands behind her and with high steps began to walk around me looking me up and down.

"You are a strong one, aren't you? Bonnie asked me as she positions herself before me.

"That I am." I replied as I also examine her image before me.

"I did not thank you for helping me last night when I was at my lowest." Bonnie said as she again continued to walk around me.

When she again faced me, she said, "You know I was not going to jump off that bridge? I had been walking and my leg had a cramp in it. I guess to you it looked like I was going to jump into the water. But, I was not. You yelled at me and my emotions over my Mother's death just hit me. You can understand that. Can't you?"

"I'm glad I could help you with your emotions." I answered while thinking, "Where she going with this."

She continued to walk around me. I followed her movement. Her slender body and the way she moves made her seem almost childish. I continued to stand still letting her beauty fill my vision.

Suddenly, she stopped her pacing in front of me. Looked

me square in the face with one eye closed. Her face slightly extended out as if she was eying me closely. Her mouth had a stern and twisted looked about it. She then said, "You're sure you didn't pick my card up last night and put it in your pocket. I just know you got it and for some reason you think if I read it, I'm going to jump off that bridge. Now, give it to me?"

"Now why would I do such a thing? Seeing that you were not going to jump off that bridge and drown yourself." I said standing my ground.

"You think your smart don't you?" she asked.

"Smart enough to ask you if you would like to go to a dance Saturday at the Top Fin Club." I replied with the biggest smile my face could hold.

My answer stunned her for a second causing her to take a step back. She then turned with a huff and headed back into the garage. Stopped, turned around and said, "And why should I go out with you?"

"Because I think you're the most beautiful girl I have ever seen and I am the most handsome and strongest boy in town is why." I answered while turning around and around with my arms outstretch.

"I'm also the best dancer you will ever see." I added as I did a jig or two.

"Well your buddy, Tom, asked me first and I told him that I would think about it." She answered "He also told me he was the most handsome guy and the best dancer in town."

"He said that did him?" I replied. "I got an idea. Why don't you get your Father to drop you off at the dance? Then dance with both of us and make your own decision just who is the best. That way, you know who the best is and I already know that will be me."

I then did a quick turn around and bowed.

She just laughed. Which made her all the more radiant as she stood with the dark garage entrance behind her?

Suddenly a voice behind her said, "She'll be there, Norman. She just loves to dance."

"Oh Daddy," She huffed as she turned and ran inside just a gigging.

"See you at the dance." I yelled as her image disappeared into the garage.

As I left the garage, her smile, her sense of humor, her girlish ways, and her beautiful body filled my mind as I wondered toward home. About halfway there I remembered tomorrow was when Gary and I usually go fishing. I wonder if he would like to go with me to the Top Fin Club. I'll pay his way into the club and buy him a drink or two. Just maybe he could find himself a girlfriend there. At least, he could support me in my effort to win Bonnie's heart. These things were wondering through my mind as I traveled home.

Three

CHAPTER

"*N*orman, Norman," brought Norman back to reality as Bonnie called to him from the bedroom doorway.

"I'm hungry. Can you fix me some bacon and eggs with toast?"

Bonnie said as she slowly entered the living room.

Norman quickly stood and with a couple steps was by her side and said, "I'll be glad to do that, Honey. Let me help you to the table."

Norman gently placed his arms around her and led her slowly toward the kitchen table. As he was leading her, he said, "You looking good this morning. How did you sleep? Good I hope."

"I don't know." She replied as she shuffled her feet toward the kitchen table with Norman walking beside her, making sure she did not fall. He did not intervene with her progress as she slowly wondered over to the kitchen table. He then helped her into her chair.

As Norman left her to fix her a cup of coffee he said, "You know Clara is coming to take you to the doctor today." "She is?" Bonnie answered.

"Yes she is." Norman said. "You have an appointment at two this afternoon and she'll be here soon."

"Ok," Bonnie said as she repositioned herself at the table. Norman became busy making her a bowl of oatmeal. Bonnie had asked for eggs and bacon this morning but Norman knew it was just her way in the morning when she woke up. She was really asking for oatmeal for she cannot remember its name. As the water was heating, he poured a cup of coffee. Added cream and sugar and placed it on the table before her. Then as he returned back to the stove he said, "Drink your coffee now and I'll soon have your favorite ready, Honey and Cinnamon."

It was not long till he had a bowl of oatmeal before her. Norman refilled his coffee cup and sat down beside her. He did not speak as he watched her eat. She ate very slowly as if savoring every bite. Letting the favor of the mixture explored in her mouth. Her hand shook as she gathered a spoon full from the bowel. Several times, Norman had to help her. He did not rush her or even attempted to advise her not to spill any. She was the love of his life. She had been good to him throughout his life ever sense he married her so many years ago. As he watched her eat, He thought,

"I almost blew it at the dance that Saturday after we met. It was all because I took Gary McGee and his twin sister along with me to the dance."

It was one of those hot muggy nights when I arrived at Gary's house. Dad let me borrow the car saying, "Bring it back just as you received it. No drinking or fighting or even let anyone in the car that smokes."

I said, "Yes Dad. I'll be careful."

I knew they worried about me or were they worried about the car. I never knew. I often borrowed it and always been careful with it. When I arrived at Gary's house, he was standing talking to Becky. He instantly grabbed her hand and walked her toward the car. She wore the most beautiful dress I've ever seen her wear. It was a light blue with dark blue lace around the fridges. She had her light brown hair pulled back with a sparkly broach holding it. Her makeup made her face very pleasing to look at. In fact, as Gary led her to the car, she was very beautiful to look at. I had taken her out to the movies several times. There had never been anything serious between us. I liked her. She had always been like a Tomboy and my best friend's sister. Right now she was quit pleasing to the eye none the lease.

"You don't mine me bringing Becky alone do you?" Gary asked as he opened the back door of the car.

"Sure," I answered. "Hello Becky, you look ravishing in that dress and I just know you will be the hit of the dance.

That is for sure." "Why Thank you, Norman." Becky replied as she entered the car.

"Gary told me you were going tonight. So, I thought, I would come alone with you. Besides, I'm not doing anything important."

"Is Gary your date or you're just hitching a ride?" I asked her as Gary closed the car door.

"Me and Gary date?" She laughed. "He's my brother and besides I'm too old for him."

"Me too old you say." Gary said as he sided himself into the front seat.

"Just because you were three minutes older than me, does not mean I'm too young to date you." Gary joked. "Being twins and the first born, does not give the right to rule over me. Mom said so."

"She didn't say that." Becky counted. "She told me as the oldest, I'm to boss you around."

Gary looked over at me for help. I just shrugged my shoulders and smiled at him. Backed the car out of the driveway and as I started down the road heading for the Gaff Fin Club I said with a laugh, "Give up Gary, she got you over a barrel and you can't win. Besides, Becky is a lot prettier then you."

"You think so?" Gary said. "I do." I replied.

We all laughed and joked as I drove the seven miles to the club. When we arrived there were many cars parked along the edge of the road. The small parking lot appeared full. I drove the car passed the Club, turned around and parked Dad's car along the edge along with the other cars.

"The Club will be crowded tonight." I said as I helped Becky out of the car.

"It looks to be that way. "Becky answered as she stood. "I hope we can find a table."

Gary quickly joined us as we walked across the road. Becky grabbed hold of my arm as we walked. Her hair broach and ear rings were sparking under the street lighting. That is when I notice Bonnie watching us from beside the entrance into the club. I started to shake out of Becky's grasp but thought otherwise. I was just being polit. Bonnie could understand that I hoped. As I walked toward the entrance, I could see Bonnie was wearing a very nice outfit with a ruffled gray skirt with black lines running through it and a solid black blouse with a slight V cut just exposing her breasts. Her hair was pulled back in a ponytail and held there by a black hair broach which sparkled when she turned her head. Seeing her standing at the entrance waiting for me made my heart yearned to take her in my arms and kiss her.

"I see you made the dance and if I may say so, you are ravishing in black." I said as I stopped before her.

"Who these two with you," Bonnie asked.

Bonnie," I answered as walked behind them and placing hands on their shoulders said, "Let me introduce the McGee's to you. This here holding my hand is Becky and the guy here is Gary. I promise to pay their way into the club tonight. Would you like for me to pay your way in also?"

"No Thanks," Bonnie said. "I've already paid." She then showed me the red stamp on her hand that they put on you when you pay the entrance fee into the club.

Becky then held her hand out to Bonnie and said, "I guess you are the girl Norman been talking all the way here about. I'm glad to meet you."

Bonnie smile saying, "I guess you are Normans' date?"

This brought a good laughed from Gary who said, "No Bonnie, she not his date. She heard we were coming here tonight and just hitched a ride."

Bonnie walked over to Gary and quickly grabbed his arm. Smiled and said, "Gary, I just would love for you to dance with me tonight. You don't mine, do you Norman?" Bonnie now had that look about her that said, you have a girl on your arm and I have a guy on mine.

I just shook my head and led Becky into the club. I had just started to pay the entrance fee for us when Tom Sneed approached us.

"Wow, you look beautiful tonight, Becky." Tom said as he grabbed Becky's free hand and pull her away from me. He then lifted her arm up into the air and spun her around.

"Are you free, are," he held the "Are" before he continued, "you Normans' date?"

Becky was blushing as she said, "I've just come to dance

is all." Tom still holding her hand said, "Well then, if you are free how about coming and sit with me. We can dance every dance. Have a few drinks and just enjoy the atmosphere of the establishment. What do you say?"

Becky was stumbling over what to say when Bonnie came to her rescue when she said, "She with us. Isn't that right Norman? You can come and asked Becky to dance from our table if she still there."

Tom started to say something when Mr. French, the Club's Bouncer interrupted and said, "Tom, Girls, move out of the doorway and take the discussing into the dance hall."

I finish paying the entrance fee and everybody had their hand marked. We then entered the hall and proceeded to fine ourselves a table. Tom, who was now sitting with Sonny and Fred, kept motioning for Becky to join them. Which Becky ignored. I smiled at Tom and there in the corner of the Hall I notice a table that could sit all of us. There was an older man at the table sitting alone drinking a beer.

As we approached the table, I asked, "Hello Mr. Roberts, do you mind if we sit with you. It appears this is the only table where we can all sit together."

He stood and said, "Sure, if I could have the first dance with either of these beautiful girls."

As we took a seat around the large table Becky remain standing saying, "Hello, Mr. Roberts."

Mr. Roberts smiled as held his hand out toward saying, "Becky,

Would you like to have this dance with me?"

"Sure," Becky answered as she took his hand and was slowly led out onto the dance floor.

"Bonnie, would you like to dance?" I asked for it was a fast song.

"Way too fast for me," Bonnie said as she sat down and placed her bag across the back of the chair.

"If not, then what would you like to drink?" I asked.

Gary interrupted us by saying, "I'll go get them and I'll buy the first round. I'm getting myself a beer."

He waited a second and none of us answered he finally louder voice said, "Norman, Bonnie?"

I was looking at Bonnie just admiring her sitting posture when she said, "Just get me a coffee. One of those with wiped cream on top which I saw one of the girls drinking as we entered the Dance Hall."

I followed with, "I'll have the same."

Gary looked at me for a second with one of his real hard looks and quietly asked, "You're drinking coffee with wiped cream on top, also"

I answered, "Yes," as he gave me another wide eyed look as he left Beth and me alone.

As I looked out across the dance floor watching the many dancers, I thought to myself, "She did join us and was waiting for me at the Dance Hall entrance when we arrived."

I returned my attention back to Bonnie. I then reached and took her hand which she allowed me to do. I held it liking the feeling of it in my hand and said, "I'm sure glad you came tonight. I'm really looking forward to dancing with you and I think you're the most beautiful girl I've ever seen."

"Now don't you go and say such things?" Bonnie said as she removed her hand from mine.

"Know, I really mean it." I countered. "I really think you're the most ravishing girl in this whole place."

"Well, if you think that? Then I think you're the handsomest fellow in this whole place." Bonnie said with a smile just before we both laughed breaking the tension that existed between us.

As she calmed down Bonnie said, "Now, that our introduction is over. How about you and I go dancing after Gary brings us our coffee?"

"How about dancing the next song they play?" I asked just as Gary arrived with our coffees with whip cream on top. He looked at us both and then without speaking, left to retrieved Becky's and his drinks.

That is when Tom appeared interrupting our conversation and said, "Hello Bonnie, you do look ravishing tonight."

"Thank you, Tom." Bonnie replied.

Tom, without asking sat down across from us and said,

"Norman, you do not mine if I sit with the two of you. Do you? I'm alone and Bonnie did promise me a dance or two. Isn't that right Bonnie?"

"That right." Bonnie answered. "How about we dance the next song? Then you and Becky can dance all the songs."

I started to interrupt her but change my mind as she stood and walked out onto the dance floor. Tom quickly stood and followed her and took her hand just before the band began to play a nice smooth Fox Trot or Two Stepped it was sometimes called.

I watched them as they began to dance. Bonnie appeared to know how to dance quite nicely as she followed Tom's lead. I looked for Becky and there on the far side of the dance floor George and Becky were still dancing together. I could see that Becky was talking his ear off which was her usually way when dancing. George would just nod and smile. I guess he was agreeing with whatever she was telling him.

I returned my attention back to Tom and Bonnie. Thou, they had turned down the overhead lights I could see them quite nicely. I watched Bonnie's dancing moves admiring her grace and charm as she moved to the music. I picked my coffee up and took a sipped, letting the coffee flavor dwell within my mouth. The sweetness of the wipe cream mixed with it gave it a very pleasant taste. "That is good." I thought.

As I was returning my attention back to Tom and Bonnie, Gary returned and set his beer and Becky's drink upon the table and sat down across from me.

"What kind of drink did you get Becky?" I asked not taking my eyes off of Bonnie's dancing.

"Shirley Temple, It's her favorite." Gary answered as he took a big drink of his beer before he said, "Way too sweet for my taste."

"Mine too" I replied.

"I see Tom's dancing with your girlfriend." Gary said as he took another drink of his beer.

"She promise him a couple dances is all." I replied. "When she comes back, I'm hoping she'll dance with me the rest of the night."

"That's good." Gary said as guzzled down the rest of his beer. "I met Judy Hensley at the bar while getting our drinks is why I took so long." Gary said as he stood. "You remember her, don't you? She played on the Girls Basketball Team and always set in front during class. I asked her for a dance and she said, "OK." I think I'll go fine her and leave you two alone."

"Gary, don't you dare get drunk." I said as I turned my complete attention to him. "I do not want to carry you to the car like I did the last time we were here."

"I'll be Ok." Gary said as he left the table. "I spent my last dollar on our drinks. There will be no drunken Gary tonight." He laughed and was just able to dodge one of the dancing couples as he left.

I watched him leave. Then I turned my attention back to Tom and Bonnie. They were now dancing under the colored lighting located in the middle of the dance floor. As the music ended, Tom gave Bonnie a twirl. They both laughed. He then led her to our table followed closely by George and Becky. Everyone was in good Spirits as they greeted each other.

As Bonnie took her seat next to me I asked, "Bonnie, I did not know you could dance like an expert. It was a joy to watch you dance with such grace and beauty."

Bonnie just smile as she took a drink of her coffee and place her other hand upon mine.

George left Becky as she took her seat across from Bonnie and he said, "I best me mosey along and let you young guys take over. It was fun dancing with you Becky." He then reached and calmly took his beer off the table, smiled and wonder back onto the dance floor as the Band began to play another Fox Trot.

As George was leaving, Becky said, "It was my pleasure to dance with such a fine gentleman as you, George. Come back and I'll dance with you anytime."

George returned, "I just might do that before the night is over."

Becky began sipping on her Shirley Temple when Tom stood asking, "Want to dance the next song, Becky."

"Sure do," she answered standing and almost pushing Tom out the upon the dance floor.

The next song was a slow waltz. I stood and without speaking motion with my hand and head for Bonnie to join me. She calmly stood and taking my hand followed me out upon to dance floor. The waltz helps to fill my heart with love as Bonnie took my other hand and we began moving with the music.

I could see a small smile was upon her face as we waltz across the floor almost as one. Whichever I turned, she followed nicely letting me do all the leading.

Without me giving any indication, she drew real close to me positioning her breasts against my chest and placing her head against my shoulder. Our dance became a slow motion with me placing the hand on her waist across her back pulling her real close against me. I felt my groin begin to glow. I just knew she felt my now ridged penis against her groin area. She moved in such away she rubbed against it. Her pressing and moving her hips caused me to close my eyes feeling the flow her body next to me. I place my head against hers. I tried not to let it appear as if we were having sex on the floor of the dance hall. I was not expecting this. I did not stop it either.

When the music stopped, we just held each other, neither wishing to let go. Neither of us was willing to return to our table. Both our groins glowing, pulsing to our heart beat. The next song was a fast two step. The song's fast pace allowed us to escape our love making we were doing on the dance floor without being notice. We just joined in with the other dancers. The fast pace allowed my groin to calmed down. By the time the song had finish, both Bonnie and I knew there was something different about our relationship that neither of us had ever experience. I knew what she wanted and she knew what I wanted.

I lead her back to our table. We spoke not a word as I held her hand as we walked. As she sat down in her chair, she looked upped at me and smiled as I gained my seat. Bonnie, took a sip of the now cold coffee admiring how the wiped cream formed a mustache across her upper lip.

Becky and Tom arrival back at the table change the atmosphere for Bonnie and me.

Tom, as he was pulling Becky's chair out to allow Becky to sit said, "You two looked like a couple love bugs on the dance floor."

"I'll say," Becky added.

Bonnie's face flushed red at their statements while she turned to me and smiled. I smiled back and squeeze her hand which I still held.

"Now you two leave us alone." I said while finishing off the last bit of my coffee. "We are just getting to know each other. Testing our environment, you might say."

Becky finished her drink, stood and said, "I'm going to the ladies' room to freshen up. Bonnie, would you like to join me?"

Bonnie let go of my hand, stood, and was soon walking beside Becky toward the ladies' room which was located near the entrance of the club. Becky stopped and pointed a finger toward me and said, "I'll take another Shirley Temple and Bonnie wants another coffee with wipe cream. You hear me Norman?"

"Yes Mam," I said as I stood to wonder over to the bar. Tom quickly joins me as we dodged dancers who were fast dancing to the beat of the song the Band was playing. I dodged one couple that was dancing wildly. But Tom could not miss them for the girl we knew as Donna Smith danced right into him.

Tom said, "Sorry."

But that was not good enough for her dance partner who was quit drunk and in slurred speech said, "What do you mean bumping into my wife?"

Now Donna, who was also drunk said, "Now Paul, he didn't mean too. In fact, I think it was I that bumped into him."

"It was not." Paul slurred. "He did it on purpose. I saw him. I just think I'm going to teach him a lesson."

"Sure you are." Donna said. "In your condition, I think he would teach you a lesson and I'll just sit back and laugh while he does it too."

Paul, who was so drunk he was staggering, walked toward Tom ready to fight saying, "Which one of you three bumped into my wife?"

Tom and I stood watching him for it was quite funny. When from behind us a voice said, "Paul, I think you had enough to drink."

That was when Mr. French walked around us and stood facing Paul. Paul realized he was in trouble slurred; "I wasn't going to do anything. Just having some fun is all. Isn't that right, Donna?"

Donna came to his rescue for now a small crowd was watching us. She grabbed whole of Paul's arm and said, "Mr. French, I'll take full responsibility of him. Keep him out of trouble."

Mr. French, Looked Paul right in the eye and with a pointing finger said, "Paul, you have three kids at home. I would hate to see you placed in the drunk tank tonight. I think I you better turned back to your table and sober up. The Bar is off limits to you as of now."

Mr. French then turned his attention to Donna, thought for a second, then said, "Donna, take Paul to your table and don't you are Paul leaved the table till you are both sober enough to drive home. Just watch the dancers and enjoy yourselves."

Tom and I were about to head toward the Bar for our drinks when I felt a tap on my shoulder and Mr. French without smiling said, "I want you two to get Paul and Donna several cokes and take them to their table. You almost cause a ruckus here. That is your punishment. I'm letting you off lightly you understand?"

Tom started to say something, when the girls appeared and Becky said, "You gotten our drinks yet?"

"Not yet" I replied as I grabbed Tom's arm and led him away saying, "We're meet you at the table."

Tom and I took Paul and Donna several cokes. Donna apologized for causing us trouble and interrupted our fun. Paul had gone asleep with his head tucked in his arms on the table. We quickly returned to the Bar and purchase our own drinks.

As we walked toward our table, we could see the girls were not there. I looked across the dance floor and there they were both fast dancing with George. I watched for second admiring both girls dance moves just before I place our coffee's on the table and sat down. I could see they were having too much fun dancing with George for me to interrupt them. I just sat and watched them danced with Bonnie looking more and more radiant as she danced before me. Her smile, her nice figure, her bouncing blond ponytail and her skirt spinning out as she turned was a joy for me to watch. Tom sat Becky's and his drink down on the table and drifted out on the dance floor and was soon fast dancing with Becky.

As I sat there and watched, the vision of Bonnie dancing gave my heart a wonderful feeling. As if it may bust at any moment with the love that was bubbling up in me for her. I have never felt this way toward any girl I've known or dated. Bonnie was diffidently different. I could not put my finger on it. I guess I was just in love with her. I thought, as I watched her dance, that I have never been in love with any girl before. No wonder men go crazy when they find the love of their life. I wonder if she feels the same way toward me. Does her heart tighten while she holding my hand? I have danced only a couple songs with her and I already felt something from her. A small indication of what the future may hold. I knew right then as I watch her dance that I'm going to marry her, and take care of her and have several kids by her and live with her the rest of my life. As I sat there watching her I knew right then that was what I was goanna do.

When the music stopped, my wondering mind settled downed as I watched Bonnie walk quickly toward me. Held out her hand and said, "Let's dance, Norman."

"Sure, "I said as I quickly stood and took her hand. Smiling, she led me out onto the dance floor and we stood holding hands waiting and watching for the band to start a new song. The next song was a slow Two Step. I felt her smoothness and grace as we began dancing to the music. While we danced, we spoke not a word to each other. We just felt each other's body movement as we danced to the songs they played. My love for her growing and growing with each dance step we took. Her strong hand in mine, her hand across my shoulder, her breasts touching my chest and often she pushed them against me. We continued to feel each other's body movement as we danced the songs the band played. It seems to me she was talking to me with her body saying, "I love you." Her eyes were always looking into mine, never leaving as I glided her across the dance floor. They talked to me saying, "I love you. I want to be with you. Make sweet love to you." I moaned deep inside of my heart whenever we waltz to a very slow song. Her closeness excited my groin. She never wavered whenever she presses her body against mine. Sometimes we continued to slow dance as they played a fast Two Step. Afraid to let go of each other, thinking with our parting it would end the closeness we felt for each other. Afraid the world would then would know what was inside our hearts and try it's best to take this feeling of love for each other plumb away from us. But deep inside, we both knew it could not last. The band will stop their playing. The lights will come on and our togetherness would be exposed. We then would have to separate and walk ourselves back to our table. Then the band did stop playing. The lights did come on and it was time for us to return to our table and cold coffee with wipe cream.

Bonnie leaned against me as we maneuvered around the many dancers as we travel to our table. I could see Tom was holding Becky's hand up close to his mouth and proceeded to kiss it. I knew our appearance would interrupt his sweet talk with Becky. She just smiled at us as we took our seats.

"Having fun are we?" I heard Gary's voice speak behind me.

I turned around and there holding hands were Judy and Gary with a cold sweating beer in their hands. A thought hit me, "I never did see Gary or Judy on the dance floor."

"We sure are." I answered. "Now where have you been? I looked for you on the dance floor. But you were nowhere to be found."

Gary said, "Judy said she can't dance and comes just to enjoy the music and atmosphere."

Judy beside him took a swig of her beer before saying, "He has been sitting with me watching the dancers. Learn a lot when you watch."

"That we do." Gary said as he shook his head in the "Yes" motion while a smile grew upon his face.

He took another swig of his beer before continuing, "We been watching Bonnie and you dance and I can tell you one thing, I'm quit empress with the performance I saw."

Judy separated herself from Gary and went over to Bonnie and said, "I'm Judy Hensley. Known these guys sense we were in grade school. I would not trust them as far as I could throw them. But, Norman here would give the shirt off his back if you need it. If you can catch him, you got a good one. That the honest truth. Let me tell you. I've known a many a girl that tried."

"Why thank you Judy," Bonnie replied. "That is the same thing Becky told me. I guess I can't go wrong if I fall in love with him, would I."

"Not even a little bit. "Judy answered.

Judy and Gary join us at the table and continued to joke over my life exploits as they knew it till the band returned from their break. I tried to ignore their good humor statements the best I could. Bonnie, seem to enjoy my torture. She kept asking questions. I just held my head down and placed my hands over it. When the band began to play again, I stood and motion Bonnie to join me on the dance floor.

She just looked up at me and said, "After what Gary, Becky, Tom and Judy have just told me, I just wonder is it safe to be on the dance floor with you."

She then kinder gave me an over her left shoulder head down look with her eyes. As if she was considering should she dance with me or not. Her lips which had been folded into her mouth slowly opened and a wonderful smile bloomed showing her pearly white teeth.

Then she said, "I guess it is safe. But, I'll only dance with you if you promise to dance every dance with me till eleven thirty. That is when Daddy to supposed to come and get me."

A big smile filled my face as I held out my hand toward her. I then said, "Bonnie, "I'll not only dance every dance with you till your Dad comes. I'll dance you right out the Club door and into his car."

A good Spirit seemed to fill the Club as Bonnie and I dance.

Couples were having fun. The band was playing great music. As I dance with Bonnie, it felt as if my body could not hold all the love I was feeling toward her. It felt as if the love I had was just flowing out of me into every soul that was on the dance floor. That wonderful, marvelous, extraordinary Spirit of love that fills one soul when a man cannot help it when he falls head over hills in love with a beautiful, gorgeous and good natured woman like Bonnie.

But, all good things must end. I did not want to. I slowly had to lead Bonnie out to her Dad's car. Each step a reminded she was leaving me. Each step I took, I wanted to kiss her, hold her, brush my hand through her hair and look into her beautiful blue eyes and tell her how much I love her. Letting go of her hand as she entered her Dad's car about killed me. As they were leaving my whole body and special my heart was beating, I love you, I love you, and I love you. I could just barely see her in the darkness waving at me through the back windshield as they left. All I could do was wave back. I stood in middle of the road watching them leave till a car's honk broke my concentration.

As I slowly wondered toward my Dad's car, a thought hit me what tomorrow will be like. Suddenly, I felt happy. So happy in fact, that I jumped into the air clicking my heels together, throwing my arms out as I did and not caring who heard me I yelled, "I'm in love."

The joy I felt as I open the door to my car was not just a joy in my heart but it was one that filled my whole body.

I mean from my head to my toes. As I open the car door could not help myself as I held onto the door and scuffled my feet to the rhythm of love that was beating in my heart. Thinking the whole time, "I'm in love."

I left driving slowly. Not wanting the feeling of love to pass and wait for me to reappear in the future when she and I meet again where I would just melt even if I even just touch her hand.

"I just got to be crazy to fill this in love with anyone." I thought trying to get my mind off of her. I even slapped myself.

That did not work as her beautiful eyes filled my vision. Her cute little smile and laughter and her hair, it felt so soft every time I was able to touch it. The way she walked letting her dress swing out from her if she turned to fast and I just knew she did that just for me.

Normal left the past and all mine could do was wonder only thinking about the love of his life being so sick and him being unable to stop it.

He shook his head sadly thinking, "My Bonnie the love of my life is getting ready to leave me. I just know she is and soon all I will have is her memories when we were active and full of gladness as we gave birth to three wonderful children. I kept us fed and joy I felt each day as I come home a table of joyful or mournful children as she rewarded or punished them. Always full of laughter and always full of stories of that day events as we went to bed each night. She was my light in my darkness allowing me to see God. She had a way about her that at times you swore she was half Ghost and half women. It brought me closer to our Lord very positive he was watching over us.

Four

"*I* fell completely in love with Bonnie that night." Norman thought as he placed her bowel in the sink. He turned and looked at his love as she sat staring out the window. She still had that radiant beauty that he fell in love with so many years ago. Although her hair was now completely white as was his, it only expresses their age. His love for her has never wavered or change.

Norman refilled his coffee cup and took a sipped as he walked over to her side and said, "Bonnie, you know you have a doctor appointment later today. I think it is time for you to take a shower and get dress for today."

Bonnie looked at him and with a blank look on her face said, "Get dress?"

"Yes Bonnie, Get dress." Norman answered. "Clara

coming to pick us up soon and we must be ready to go with her."

Norman then gently pulled her chair out from the table and said, "You want me to help you or do you want to do it by yourself?"

Bonnie did not answer him as she stood. She looked at Norman and said, "We're going to the Doctor? Who's sick?"

"There is no one, Bonnie, No one." Norman answered said as he took her hand. "We're going for a checkup is all? Now let me help you walk into our bedroom. We will walk real slowly as not to stumble and fall."

Norman allowed Bonnie to slowly shuffle her way toward the bedroom. He did not interrupt her movement unless she appeared to have trouble. Which to his delight, she didn't. Usually Norman used the wheelchair which made it easier to move her around. But, Norman has found if he gave her a little independence in the morning, Bonnie would often dress herself without his help. He also knew it did not always work.

He followed her into the bedroom saying as they entered, "I think you should take a shower first."

"I think so." Bonnie said as she continued toward the bathroom. Once inside, Norman helped her to remove her night gown and depends which was full of pee. He did not say anything for he knew it was just part of his job after refusing to place her in a Home.

Her naked body did not have the plumpness she had when they first met. Sickness and being unable to eat at times has taken its toll on her. He could see her ribs and her breasts were no longer firm. She had so much change of what she was that Norman would sit and cry while she slept.

Every day Norman was praying to God, that he would allow him to hold her one more day like he done over the years. Norman always asked, "Lord, Just one more day and would he give him the strength and the chance to see her as she was so many years ago."

Norman took his clothes off and entered the shower stall with her and helped her to sit onto the shower's chair, adjusted the water temperature, before allowing the warm water to flow over her and him. He had found this was the best way to clean her by both of them to taking a shower together. He did mostly also for safety for unless he watched her closely she would turn the knobs and could possibly make the water way to hot and possible scaled her.

Norman slowly began to wash her starting with her lower legs and moving upward. He washed her groin area then move upward. She stopped him for a second when he reached her breasts. He remembered that they were very sensitive to his touch. She just loved for him to lick them when they made love. Norman always felt it was his job to please her. Letting her enjoy the pleasure of her body as he touches and kissed her. Now only when he washes her does she appear to have any pleasure at all. But, there was a time when she often was the aggressor in their love making. As he continues to wash her, he started to reflex back to their first real sexual encounter. As he remembered, he felt the old familiar glow in his groin.

That was after I started working for Mr. Sisk that Monday after the dance. He put me to doing odd jobs like cleaning parts he pulled giving me their names forcing me to memorize them. As I worked I often would have asked him how Bonnie was doing. He always answered, "Just fine, pretty as ever."

I did not dig any farther after asking. But my mine was on her all week. I tried calling her. There was either no answer or Mr. Sisk would answer telling me she over at the neighbors. After three days of working, I knew I needed transportation of some type. Dad used his car for work and would only allow me to use it on weekends when they were doing nothing or going nowhere.

I started looking in the Newspaper or on the advertisement board at the local grocery store on my home from work. There was always nothing listed I could afford.

Without any type of transportation but my size twelve feet, Saturday morning I took off walking toward her house. I had gone only to the edge of town when Mr. Sisk and Bonnie appeared in their Dodge Pickup. Bonnie waved at me and Mr. Sisk nodded as they passed by me. Mr. Sisk did not stop but just drove right on while

Bonnie continuing waving at me through the back window.

I started to run after them. For some reason, Mr. Sisk just kept right on driving into town. I could see Bonnie waving and laughing as I ran after them. Darn if he not teasing me I thought as I trotted along. I could feel my legs stiffness as I ran. I've been too tired when I got home from work to have my usual late night excursions across town and now my legs were screaming "Stop". I slowed down to a walk for I was now breathing quit heavy from my initial excursion to catch them.

I could see Mr. Sisk had turned into Wall to Wall Grocery Store. "I guess their getting some groceries," I thought as I walked along. After a few minutes I felt my heart beat slow down to a normal beat. I then picked up my pace till I was traveling along at a trot. As I neared the store, I could see Bonnie standing beside the truck waiting for me. A large smile was across her face. In the Sun Light with the Gulf breezed gently blowing her hair she looked all the more charming. I smile back at her.

I slowed to a walk as I got close and Bonnie said, "That was mean of Daddy was it not. He said you needed the exercised."

"I think he is trying to keep us apart." I said as I stopped before her.

"It is not him it's me." Bonnie said as she suddenly reached out and wrapped her arms around my sweaty neck.

"You were the one?" I asked with a puzzled look upon my face as I looked deeply into her blue eyes as I slowly removed her arms away

and said, "I'm all sweaty right now."

"I don't care if I get wet." Bonnie said. "And "Yes," It was me. I'm been just afraid to jump into any relationship. Specially, with someone I know I'm in love with."

"Really," I said, "You are scared I would break your heart and all the while I'm thinking you will break mine. I can tell you one thing. I'm deeply in love with you and that is the truth."

Bonnie, as she leaned backed against the truck bed wiping my sweet off her arms onto her dress she said, "Daddy likes you. He also told me I was old enough to make my own decisions and if I wanted to go out with you, he was ok with that."

"He said that?" I asked as I position myself against the truck beside her.

"Yes he did." Bonnie said as moved closer to me.

I wiped the sweet off my face with the now drench shirt sleeve and said, "Sorry I got you all wet. Besides that, running here after you in this heat has also made me quite thirsty. Would you like a soda? I think I'll get me one from the vending machine over there by the door."

"Why don't you take your shirt off and let me see all your muscles?" Bonnie jokingly said as she followed me over to the Soda Pop Vending Machine.

"Not here in the parking lot. I'm not." I said as I placed a dime to get a Soda Pop.

"I was wondering, how about we go swimming or something?" Bonnie asked as she walked backwards toward truck, turned and reach into the truck through the window and brought out a swimsuit. Then without hesitation, she placed it across her body allowing me to visualize her in it.

I looked at her as I place another dime in the Vending Machine for another soda for us.

Bonnie lean backed against the truck and said, "You think I would look nice in it all wet lying on the beach somewhere?"

"That it would," I said as I handed her a cold soda. "But, I would have to go home and fetch mine."

"Already solved," Bonnie answered as she reached back into the truck and brought out a nice multicolored man's swim trunks.

"You see. I've thought of everything." Bonnie said with a laugh as she placed the trunks across my waist to see if they fit. I just smile as she measured me. Just admiring her sense of hummer and how it was she was not bashful even a little bit about her speaking her mine what she wanted.

"Why are you doing this?" I asked. "Want your dad get real mad or something, if I just run off with you and not tell him where we are going?"

"He knows already because I told this morning what we were going to do." Bonnie answered.

"What do you mean he already knows?" I asked leaning toward her looking at her out the corner of my eyes.

Bonnie just shuffled her feet sliding her right foot then to her left thinking of an answered. She looked at me and as she spoke her face turned a little red she said, "I told Daddy I was going to marry you and what I do with you is my own business. I also told him that I'm over eighteen, out of school and almost on my own. I told him I have met a young man that loves me that I trust him, and I love him with all my heart. I also told him, he loves me also. So there, is not a good enough answer?"

"What did he say then?" I asked drawing closer to her.

Daddy said to me, "Bonnie, you are grown women now. I've known for a long time you were going to leave me when you found someone special. If you love Norman, then go and be with him. Treat him as your Mother treated me. Love him and show him your love with all that is within you."

"Why did you not answer my calls?" I asked now leaning against the truck beside her.

"I needed time to think is why." Bonnie answered. "I wanted to be alone and figure out my heart. You see I never have felt this way toward anyone before. I guess now that I look back, I've never been in love before. I studied my heart and with the help of Daddy came to the conclusion I wanted you for with all heart I know you will take care me. For you have already shown me compassion when you held me on the bridge. You are a kind and gentle man. I know with all my heart you will love me till the day I die. It is not something I've learn from being with you. It is what I know in my heart to be true. You love me as much as I love you."

I could see a few tears forming in her eyes as she said, "You believe me do you not?"

Bonnie then stepped away from the truck side and faced me with her tear stained face and said, "Is that a good enough reason?"

Tears were now in my eyes also as I said, "Bonnie, I can see both of us have questioned our feeling and looked into our hearts. Testing this crazy feeling making sure our hearts are not lying to us. I have also never felt this way toward anyone my whole life. I can't sleep. I can't do anything without dreaming of you even while working at your Dad's shop."

I then took Bonnie into my arms and said, "I can tell you this. I will with all my strength will take care of you and our children till the day I die. I promise you this, right here where we stand, I love you. I know we both have our concerns. I know we are both afraid of failure. I know we are hoping for the best and I been thinking will she love as much as I love her. I can only tell you I do not know what tomorrow may bring. I guess time will only tell?"

I let go of her and held her arm's length and said, "Because to me, there will be those around us who will question our decision to marry after only knowing each other for less than two weeks. There will be those that say we are fools. I believe it was love at first sight. You believe that do you not?"

"Yes, that is exactly what I mean." Bonnie said as she came into me and we kissed. As she stepped back away from me and steadfastly said, "It is Love at first sight."

Bonnie then handed me the swimming trunks and said, "Now that we are going to get married, let's go swimming."

I wiped the tears in my eyes and took the swim trunks and said, "The best swimming area is about a mile out of town down the bayou. I usually row out to it. It is like my own private little beach you might say. We'll take Dad's boat, grabbed couple towels from the house and let's not forget about something to drink and some kind of snack."

"Let's go then?" Bonnie said as she twirled around. "It sounds like it will be lots and lots of fun."

"Wait a minute, Bonnie." I said as we left the store and crossed the street just dodging an incoming car.

"How are you going to get home?" I said as I quickly jumped in front of her while walking backwards.

"I'm not." Bonnie answered. "I'm spending the night with Becky.

But, I would love to spend the night with you. Only if you behave yourself like kiss me for hours on end."

"Yea, I'll just do that." I countered. "And I guess you'll sleep naked too."

"Maybe I will and I maybe I'll not." Bonnie said as she smiled and took hold of my hand I held out toward her.

Bonnie and I continued to discuss our future as we walked toward my Mom and Dad's house. When we arrived, Mom and Dad were just getting ready to leave to visit Uncle John and Aunt Eva. Mom put down the cake she was carrying and just had a fit over Bonnie.

"So your Norman's girlfriend that had him pacing the floor all week over?" Mom asked.

"Yes Mam, I am." Bonnie replied.

"Well it so nice to meet you, finally." Mom continued. "Norman has told us all about you and I've never seen him so excited about any girl as he become over you."

Suddenly, the screen door slam and Dad came down the stairs carrying a large box to take to the car. Saturday was their card game night sense I could remember. When he saw Bonnie he smiled and said, "Norman, is that Bonnie the girl you been telling us about all week?"

Mom answered, "Yes, it is. Isn't she a doll?"

Dad set his box down and held out his hand saying, "Well, I'm sure glad I finally get to meet you. Norman has been talking our ears off about you."

"He has?" Bonnie said looking over at me.

Dad pick upped the box he had been carrying and said, "Well, I'm very glad to meet you. After all Norman told us about you, I think I know you already. I can say one thing about him if you marry him? He will take care of you. If he doesn't, I will come and beat the Hell out of him, want I son?"

"That you will, Dad." I answered.

Mom gathered the few things she had been carrying and said, "We got to be going. Uncle John and Aunt Eva supposed to meet us at church. Their having a yard sale this afternoon and your Dad and me supposed to help them. I have a few things to add to it. The money we collect supposed to help Charles Sutton pay his hospital bill."

Daddy said, "You know him? He the one that fell through his roof while trying to fix a leak and did not realized it was rotten. Broke one of his legs and who knows what."

Mom, as she opened the car door said, "I'm so glad to have met you, Bonnie. But, we got to go."

Dad set the Boxed in the trunk and just before he entered the car he asked, "By the way, what are you two planning to do this afternoon?"

"We were thinking going swimming down at Sandy Point." I answered.

"Norman, make sure you keep her out of the Sun." Daddy said, "I would hate for her to get Sun Burn. There is a tarp and some sticks with it that you can make a lean too out of in the shed. Remember to put it back just like you got it now."

Mom said, "There also an umbrella beside the door that she can used while riding the boat."

As they left, Bonnie and I waved till they were well down the road while holding hands.

Suddenly, Bonnie gently took hold of my other hand and slowly drew me close to her. As we met, I pressed my mouth to hers. As we kissed, I closed my eyes and concentrated completely upon the feeling of our tongs as they rubbed each other. I also felt my groin beginning to have that familiar glow about it. We stood kissing like that for what seem and eternity. I did not want to let her go. But somehow with mutual consent we parted.

"Wow, I have never been kissed like that." I said as I touched her lightly upon her cheek.

Bonnie smiled as she slipped out of my arms. Picked her swimsuit and some other cloths she had been carrying from off the guard rail and proceeded upped the stairs saying, "Get the boat ready. I'm changing into my swimsuit.

I pushed the row boat into the water and tied it to the pier. Entered the shed and collected several cold sodas from the cooler, placed them in the ice chest and added ice. Collected the small tarp and poles along with a hammer to beat the poles into the sand and place them in the boat side. When I was done, I returned to the shed and changed into my swim trunks. Grabbed several towels and gathered my cloths along with sun tan lotion and anything else I thought we might need.

I place them into the boat and was just wiping out the seats of any dirt I saw when Bonnie appeared walking slowly down the stairs. All I could do was stared at her as she walked toward me. She was the most ravishing young women I have ever seen. Over her swimsuit she wore a laced see through outfit. She wore it open allowing it to hang just below her bare knees exposing her fine physique and beautiful facial fixtures. Mom's umbrella was spinning upon her shoulder outline her beautiful blond hair which was slightly fluttering in the soft gulf breeze.

I could not help myself as I let out a long soft whistle as she wondered down the stairs and upon the pier. I quickly exited the boat and with the biggest smile my face could hold I said, "Wow, you are beautiful."

As she approached me I reach and gently took her hand. With her other hand she ran it over my bare chest and down across my flat belly. Looked into my eyes and said, "Well, do you know you're the most marvelous creature I've ever seen?

I gently pulled her to me and we kissed. But, this time she ran her hands up and down my bare back which I copied. I continued to let her lead in the hand touching as our tongs rubbed each other. My groin was morning. I let go of her. Took a deep breath and said, "I think that is enough for right now. If we keep kissing like that I think I'll explore."

"That was nice wasn't it?" Bonnie said as she let go of my hand and began to enter the boat.

I stopped her and said, "Where are your clothes? If you start to sun burn, you will have need of them."

"There just inside the kitchen door." Bonnie answered.

I ran up the stairs which allowed my groin to regain its relaxed state. As I entered the kitchen I remembered there was some left over fried chicken in the fridge. But first I went into my room and gather myself a few things. In the kitchen I notice Mom had made cookies which I put into a paper bag. Collected the chicken also in another paper bag, picked upped her clothes and put them in a paper bag along with mind.

When I exited the house I could see Bonnie had already entered the boat and was waiting for me. She smiled as I handed her the bags and said, "Do you want me to row?"

I laughed and said, "I'll do that. You just sit back and enjoy the ride.

If you get hungry I found some cookies and chicken for us."

When I entered the boat I place them in the ice chest. Untied the boat and took a seat at the oars. Bonnie reached into the ice chest and took out a coke.

As Bonnie popped the capped, she asked, "Is where we going far?" "Not far." I answered as I began to row. "There a dredged canal up ahead we'll use it to cross over to Sandy Point. Years ago there was a disputed over who own the land here. It was a big court case I heard. When it was all done, the owners chose to dig a canal separating their properties. I guess that way in the future their ancestors would always know who owns what."

Where does this bayou enter the bay anyway?" Bonnie asked.

I stopped rowing and reach into the cloths bag and took out a tee shirt as I answered, "About two are three miles I think not long anyway. It opens into a shallow lake they call Gaff's lake which is also filled with oysters."

"Ever go fishing there with your Dad?" Bonnie asked as she placed her hand upon my bare leg.

"Not without a power boat for its way too far to row." I answered as I returned back to my rowing.

As I rowed, I watched her as she observed the passing shore line. Her hand was in the water letting the water flow threw her fingers. Every once in a while she moved the umbrella on her shoulder or took a drink of her soda. The gulf breeze fluttered her hair making her all the more beautiful. We did not speak as I rowed. The only sound other than the calls of the shore birds was the squeak of my oars as I dipped them into the water.

I felt the heat of the sun on my shoulders and refection of the sun from off the water. I was now very glad I darn a hat and t-shirt before I left the house. As we traveled we spoke not a word letting her enjoy the passing shore line. While my thoughts were on her beauty as she sat before me at the end of the boat. She wore a smile and every now and then she would look at me. The smile would then increase filling her lovely face. There also appear to be a sparkle in her eyes which I could not read. I just rowed with my heart overflowing with such a feeling that I was sure my God above could feel it.

It was not long till I turned into Jacob's Canal. I let the outgoing tide carry us down the canal only using the oars if our direction took us toward the bank. As we neared the opening into the bay, I could hear over the wind the choppy waters of the bay hitting Sandy Point.

"Hang on, Bonnie" I said as we entered the rough waters of the bay and I began to roe faster.

The bay waters were rough. But not rough enough to hinder me as I maneuvered the boat toward and onto the sandy shore of Sandy Point. I quickly jump out of the boat when it hit a ground and pull it a little way upon the beach. There was a nice Gulf breeze blowing. I just stood still for a second with my eyes close letting the wind cool me off from the exertion I had to use while rowing.

I stood like that till I heard, "Well, you going to help me out of the boat are not?"

"Sorry," I said as I open my eyes to see the most beautiful creature standing with her hand out to me.

As I helped her out of the boat I said, "Bonnie, have you ever just stood still while facing the Gulf breeze letting all of life's tension just fly away with it?"

"No, I have not." Bonnie answers as she stepped out of boat and stood beside me.

"Try it." I said. "Just face the wind, close your eyes and lift up your arms anyway you choose. It is one of the greatest pleasures your ever fill in your whole life.

Bonnie did as I said. I watched. Her Hair was fluttering behind her in the breezed. A small smile filled her face as she rock back and forth filling how the wind rushed by her. Its smell and the only sound were the waves and gulls calling above. I did not disturb her as she felt for the first time one of Gods greatest creations.

When she opened her eyes Bonnie said, "Your right. I never felt so alive in my whole life. That was to me an enjoyment I would like to do every time I fill blue. But right now I fill like going swimming."

Bonnie folded her umbrella and placed it into the boat. Took off her laced jacket, threw her sandals from off her feet and ran splashing into the water's edge yelling, "Come on Norman. I want to swim.

Hurry up?"

I threw my hat into the boat and my t-shirt and soon was running and splashing with her.

We went deeper and deeper into the water. Bonnie would splash me and I would splash back one time we splashed each other so fast that I could not see her for all the flying water. We laughed and yell things like, "Hee, Hee, you missed me" or "I bet you can't catch me?" or "Darn your hide. I'll get you for that."

Bonnie and I played in the water till I could feel we

needed out of the sun which I told her so. Bonnie sat down at the water edge letting the waves rush over her legs smiling upped at me as she began to make a sand castle.

As she played along the edge of the water, I constructed our lean to. Spread the blanket under it. Set the ice chess beside it. When I was satisfied all was in order, I took Bonnie by the hand and lead her out into the water saying, "Ok Bonnie, it best we get out the sun right now. We can go back later just before we head back home. First we must get all the sand off of us."

Bonnie let go of my hand and with a slap on the water sent it upon me. I splash back and soon we were again wild splashing each other and just a hallooing. But, it was not long till our now wet bodies were lying upon the blanket with each of us claiming, "I got you more then you got me."

"Want a soda?" I asked as Bonnie reposition herself upon the blanket.

"Yes, Please." Bonnie answered with a big smile. Her beauty before me was overwhelming. Her posture filled my heart with admiration as I looked at her wet body and her hair all wet and spread out behind her head as she lay on the blanket.

"Now that was a grand castle you built until a wave wash it away."

I said as I handed her a cold soda.

"You think so?" Bonnie answered as she took a good long drink of her soda.

When she was done she said, "I built it thinking of us. That it was our castle and I was the Queen and you were the King.

"I did not know you were so talented." I said as I stretch out beside her.

As I turned where I could face her, Bonnie grabbed my head, pulled it to her and we kissed. As our mouths met, her tong began reaching into my mouth for my tong. I pushed out with my tong till I was in her mouth. My eyes were closed all the while we wildly kissed each other. I slowly placed my hand upon her belly and ran it upped and down her body. Catching a touch of her breasts and out and down across her groin and out onto her legs. She seen to kiss me harder and was soon running her hand across my chess and onto my face and back down my body.

As we touched each other, my love for her exploded within me. A love I have never felt before. It was a new feeling that seems to start in my pulsing groin and travel all the way across my being. It consumed me. I felt weak and wanted to hug her so hard it knew I would hurt her. I pulled my mouth from hers and rolled over letting my excited body calm down. I was about to explode from the immense feeling of love I was feeling for Bonnie at the moment. Love that was so strong, I felt consumed by it as if I was another person and not myself.

Bonnie followed me and rolled onto her side and continued to run her hand over my body feeling the muscles in my arms. I lay motionless as she slowly ran her hands move to my chest and work downward till she felt my hardened penis. She reached and undid the knot that held my swimsuit upped and reached into them feeling my groin area. She first felted and messaged my pulsing penis feeling the wetness that flowed from its tip. She then moved her hand downward slightly squeezing each of my balls. She pulled her hand from my trunks before lifted her body over me and kissed me allowing our tongs to continue to rub each other.

Her hand remained upon my chest as she lifted herself upon her elbow and said, "I would like to do something if it is alright with you?" "Sure." I said. "Why should it not be?"

Bonnie rolled off me and began undoing the straps holding her swimsuit upped. Leaned back and slowly began worked her swimsuit off herself. I just watched as her firm rounded tits were exposed and only could smile as her groin area also appeared. The hair above her slit was very similar to the blond hair on her head but a little darker.

Bonnie then reached and slowly removed my swim trunks exposing my hard penis and groin area.

Bonnie began to explore my groin area. Lifting my penis and feeling the wetness at its head as she pulls upped on it. As she fondled my balls, Bonnie said, "I've never touched one of these before. It is quit smooth to the touch and in my eyes, it is quite beautiful."

"I would not say that myself." I replied.

"Of course not silly, you are a man and I am a woman." Bonnie countered as she slowly squeezed one of my balls.

"I can see when I pull up on it, wetness comes out. That must be the fluid that carries the sperm into me that causes babies. Isn't it?" "Yes it is." I answered. "There a lot more inside of me waiting to explode out of me. Your touching me excites me and believe me it does feel wonderful.

"It does?" Bonnie said as she slowly moved my foreskin back and forth over my red penis head liking the feel and sensation it gave her.

Bonnie bent over and kissed it and said, "I've wanted to touch and play with a boys thing ever sense I was old enough to know we were different. Mother made me promise to save myself till I met a man that would take care of me all the days of my life. I know I have found him. Now, I no longer have to save myself"

Bonnie then let go of my penis and slipped herself on top me giving me a quick kiss. Then she rolled off upon her back.

She smiled upped at me and said, "Your turn."

I rolled myself onto my side and studied her profile beside me. Her tits were moving as she breathed. Her flat belly and a slightly enter belly button presented me with a lovely image of her groin area which she exposed with open legs. I gentle felt of her firm tits. Her nipples were almost skin color. As I ran my finger around and around the nipple, the nipple tip seemed to become harder and harder. I bend over and ran my tong across her nipple feeling the nipple hardness. Bonnie morn and said, "You know they are very sensitive. I think I could just explode as you touch them."

"They are nice." I said as left them and wonder down her belly to her hair above her groin. I pull and petted the blondest hair as she opened her legs until her groin was completely exposed. I sat up and move myself around till I was facing her open legs. I opened the lips exposing the inner parts.

"Let me tell you about my pussy." Bonnie said.

Bonnie took my hand that still was rubbing her groin hair and moved my fingers until she had just one finger. She then ran my finger hand down into her pussy and said, "Feel my lovely hole. That is where your fine penis enters me."

"I know that." I said.

"It name is vagina." Bonnie said as she moved my finger upward. "Now just above it is my peeing hole." Bonnie said.

I look closely and sure enough I could see what could be a peeing hole. When look back toward her face I could see her eyes were close.

"Now above that is really my sensitive area." Bonnie

said as she moved my finger slowly upward. As she did I felt a small bump near the middle? She let go of my finger and begin to morn as I continued to feel around her pussy.

I like it." I said as I pushed my finger way into her vagina. Bonnie sat upped and kissed me saying, "You want to make me real happy. Don't you?" "Yes, I do." I answered.

"Lick it and I will have the greatest organism ever." Bonnie said as she lay back down. "I rub myself sometimes is how I know. I have given myself as many as three organisms with each one stronger than the one before."

"You have?" I asked as I continued to fondle her pussy. Thought for a second, then laid upon my stomach and maneuvered my head such I could insert my tong into her pussy. I thought it would taste bad but to my surprise it really had no taste at all. More like licking her skin I explored her pussy moving my tong from her vagina to the top of her opening. I felt the bump and concentrated my licking there before moving downward into her vagina. As I licked, I soon felt her tense as she climaxed and moaned. I did not stop. I continued a little longer licking and thought as I felt of her vagina, what the inside would feel like with my penis.

I left her pussy and slowly moved upward and licked her right breast tit. Bonnie moaned as I did. I move to her left breast and moved toward her mouth. As I did, I tried to insert my penis into her vagina. I missed I kept lightly pushing till I felt her hand take hold of it and gently helped me to insert. As I did, I moaned for the sensation was tremendous. I kept moving my hips up and down feeling my penis slowly move up and down in her. The sensation grew and grew till I felt myself about to explode. I quickly remove my penis before it did and rolled off of her.

I moved back downward thinking, "Oh Boy, better not do that. If she became pregnant it would ruin everything."

I licked Bonnie's left then right breasts just before I moved back down onto her pussy. But this time I tasted our wetness from our love making. I ignored it as I returned to licking her small nipple area above her vagina. Again she moaned but this time she moved her hands down upon my head and pushed me away. I fought her for a second getting in a few more licks before letting her push me away. As I sat up, I watched her facial expression as she slowly clammed down from her sexual pleasure I had giving her. My penis was still pulsing as I rolled off her and took a position beside her upon my back. As I did, I was thinking that was fun and pleasurable.

After a second or two, Bonnie regained her composure and said, "That was wonderful, Norman. I think I could have that happen to me every day, Thank you, Thank you, and Thank you."

Bonnie then rolled over on her elbow and kissed me.

As I fondle one of her breasts, I said, "I thought of shooting off in you. But if I did and you become pregnant, it would just ruin everything for us."

"Well, then let me do you then." Bonnie said as she reached over and started fondling my pulsing penis. She moved my skin up and down over my reddest penis head. As she did, a whitest liquid oozed out which she felt moving it across my penis head. When she did, I tensed for the sensation was almost more than I could handle. She moved to my balls studying them with her fingers.

Bonnie lowered herself and took hold of my penis with her mouth and began to suck it. Her motion sent a sensation of pleasure throughout my body as she did. I closed my eyes letting the feeling she was giving me grow and grow till I said, "It going. It is going."

Bonnie removed her mouth from off my penis and watched my joy as I ejaculated across my belly. She felt of the liquid. I watched her as she examined it with her fingers before she said, "It is quit white and causes my finger tips to move without any resistance. So this is the liquid that has all the ingredients to make me pregnant. I guess it loaded with sperm."

Bonnie took the edge of the blankets and wiped the liquid off my belly. As she did she said, "Did you know your penis gets real hard just before you organism. I really enjoyed sucking your thing and to me it is quite beautiful to look at."

"I still not sure I would say that," I answered.

Bonnie then began to fondle my now mostly limped penis.

Suddenly, Bonnie lowered her mouth upon it. I tensed for the sensation was quit pleasurable. Bonnie again started to suck it letting my penis grow hard in her mouth. I closed my eyes.

Five
CHAPTER

*N*orman finished drying Bonnie off. Hung the towel upon the shower rod and slowly led Bonnie into the bedroom allowing her to sit upon the edge of the bed. He gathered the cloths she would be wearing and set them beside her. First, he pulled the diaper up around her waist while getting her to stand. He continued the procedure of dressing Bonnie one piece of clothing at a time.

As he was slipping her bloused over her head, Bonnie asked, "Am I going somewhere Norman?"

"Yes, you are going to the doctors, Bonnie." Norman answered as he straightens the bloused across her.

"I am?" Bonnie said.

"Yes and Clara be here soon to take us." Norman said as he handed her a hair brush.

"She'll be bringing Freddy with her." Norman added

as he helped her to start brushing her hair. Which was the only thing Norman could get her to do by herself? It does not always work.

Bonnie looked into the mirror Norman had place on the wall beside the bed. Then slowly began to brush her snow white hair preparing it for the pony tail she had worn most of her life. Norman did not rush her as she performed this task. Norman always liked her pony tail and he had known for a long time that is why she always wore one. It was not for her it was for him.

But lately, it was the only task Norman could even get her to do.

He would just sit and watched. He never intervened or even any helpful comments while she brushed. At times, Bonnie facial expressions almost returned back to her former self as she slowly brushed her hair.

Norman just smiled remembering how beautiful she looked when they were married. Even now as Norman look at her, Norman could see the radiant beauty she had when He placed the wedding ring upon her finger. Looking upon his love under his breath said, "I married her almost three months to the day after we first met." Slowly his mind wondered back to when he married her as he watches her calmly and slowly comb her hair thinking, "It was almost three months after I first fell in love with her on the bridge we were married. By time, I was on full salary and was able to fix almost all the problems I faced without Mr. Sisk help. Often he would leave and visit some of his kin folks or whatever leaving me completely in charge of the garage. I did not mine. It also gave Bonnie and me time to be alone.

I remember children often came up in our conversation. The more we talked about it the more it became apparent we just had to get married. We wanted to after the first month. But, Mom and Dad and Mr. Sisk had asked us to wait. Both were saying we needed to prepare for the future. That we had to support ourselves and our children is basically what they hounded us with.

Bonnie went to work at Grace's Hamburgers and Malts. Our two incomes soon gave us enough money to buy a used car which I make almost new at the shop during my time when I had no work.

Mr. Sisk and my parents gave Bonnie and me fits. Mr. Sisk would take me around after work to look at different houses that were for sale. I would tag alone, sometime with Bonnie and sometimes without her. We would look at this one or that one. I could see as we looked, I could not even attempt to purchase any of them until we visited old man Franks house. At least that was I known him by all my life. He was located about five miles inland on ten acres of cleared land.

Old man Franks was sitting in a rocking chair on his porch when we arrived. I've known him most of my life and as I walked toward the porch I said, "Hello Mr.

Franks. You are looking chipper today." "That I am young Norman that I am." Mr. Franks said as he continued to rock watching us as we climbed the short stairs and took a seat in one of the other chairs located around the pouch.

"Here some fresh shrimp Dad sent you." I said as I placed the shrimp wrapped in newspaper upon the table.

"Why Thank you, Norman." Mr. Franks said while still rocking. "You are welcome," I answered.

As Mr. Sisk took he seat beside Mr. Franks he said, "We come to look at your house. Mr. Frank. We heard you have it for sale. Thought we would just come by and look it over if it is alright with you?" "Be my guest." Mr. Franks said pointing toward the open front door.

As I started to enter the house I asked, "You coming, Mr. Sisk?" "Norman, you go ahead and look. I think I'll sit here and talk with

Mr. Franks," Mr. Sisk answered with the biggest smile his face could hold.

As I enter the house I was thinking Mr. Sisk seem awful please about something. I didn't dwell long on that thought as I began examine the living room. The floor was uneven indicating the house needed leveling. His furniture was ragged and dusty. The plaster located on many of the walls was cracked and below the windows I could see they had leaked and the plaster was badly damage. When I entered the kitchen, I was thinking it would be a mess also. But to my surprise it was well kept. Only the cabinets needed painting.

The house had three bedrooms. Two of the rooms were closed and when I looked in, I could see Mr. Franks had clean the room, closed the door and had probably never entered again. The bathroom was well kept like the kitchen and so was the room he slept in. It appeared only the rooms he used did Mr. Franks made sure they were cleaned.

I went out the back door and walked around the house. There was rotten wood here and there along with peeling paint. I had been often to his house and I never noticed how unkempt the outside was. The more I looked, the more I dreamed that Bonnie and I just maybe could afford Mr. Franks house and land. I could fix it upped and our children would have a great place to grow up at. Land for them to play on and if I was smart enough, I could grow produce to sale and eat.

I wondered over to the out building and like the house they needed repair from neglect. One was just a storage shed for yard tools. The other was locked. Under the overhand an old black pickup was parked with all of the tires flat. Behind the locked shed I could see an old tracker that I bet had not been started in a coon's edge. There were several attachments scattered among the weeds. I also noticed the fences need mending.

I started back toward the house and notice that the six large pecan trees were loaded with pecans. I turned and wondered out into the over grown field and stood looking back at the house. The guff wind was blowing and I just closed my eyes letting the wind rock me. My mind was feeling the love God had for me as he touched me with his soft touch. I cried.

I regain my composure and as I returned to the front porch my heart was jumping with excitement. I did not know the asking price. I was hoping it was in the range I could afford.

As I took a seat beside Mr. Franks he said, "Well, what did you think of my fine house?"

"It needs lots of repair and tender care is all." I answered.

"That it does for sure." Mr. Franks said. "I have gotten too old to keep it up. It needs a young man like you is all? With a little work the place could look like new."

Suddenly, Mr. Sisk stood and shook Mr. Frank's hand saying, "I'll be in touch."

"Let us go, Norman." Mr. Sisk said as stepped off the porch and headed for his truck. I followed saying, "Glad to have met you Mr. Franks and be seeing you."

"That you will, Mr. Sisk." Mr. Franks returned.

On the way back to town, Mr. Sisk did not say a word until we were back at the garage. When he pulled into the driveway he said, "Get in your car and follow me home. I have something to tell you but not without Bonnie listening.

I followed him to his house. Not to close for the gravel

road was dry and dusty. As I pulled into his drive, Mr. Sisk was already entering the house. My mine was racing and wondering why he had to talk to both Bonnie and me. I entered and Bonnie greeted me with a smile and a raised finger to her lips telling me to be quiet. I've been in their house dozens of times sense Bonnie and I been together. Mr. Sisk was waiting for us at the kitchen table drinking a cup of coffee he had freshly poured.

"Both of you have a seat." Mr. Sisk said pointing with his free hand to the chairs around the table.

As we took our seats, Bonnie said, "Daddy, what so important you had Norman follow you home?"

"I have good news for both of you is why." He said before taking another drink of his coffee looking at us over the cup as he drank.

We waited holding hands.

Mr. Sisk set his cup down and was smiling as he said, "Mr. Franks heard you were looking for a place in which you two could live in after you were married. Yesterday, after you left and I were closing the shop, Mr. Franks stopped by and told me he would like to sale his property."

Bonnie started to interrupted him, but he said, "Hold on Bonnie.

You can ask questions later. Let me finish my story first."

Mr. Sisk took another drink of his coffee then said, "Now was I? Oh Yea. Now Mr. Franks heard you were looking for a house for sale and stopped by the shop as I was closing yesterday. He told me he wanted to sale his house and land and he wanted to sale it to young Norman. He told me he was eighty-six and as you saw today, no longer able to maintain the property. He told me he had known young Norman all his life. He said Norman always brought him fried fish, boiled shrimp or crabs not counting oysters. He said Norman always told him that his Mom and Dad were sending them to him but he knew better. He had kept a record of each time Norman took him the fried fish and such and had determined if he had to pay for such fine food he owed Norman over five hundred dollars. He knew Norman would never take money so he decided when it was time in which he could no longer live alone he would sale his property to Norman and everything on it for seven hundred dollars minis the five hundred he owed Norman. Which leaves only two hundred dollars Norman owes him? He told me that was enough money to lay him to rest and that was all he wanted."

I stood and said, "Mr. Sisk that not true. Mom and Dad were always sending our extra fried fish and broil shrimp and crabs to him. It was not me."

Mr. Sisk said, "I think he knew that. I think it is just his way of giving you a home without actually giving it to you."

Bonnie said, "Daddy, you mean he has actually giving us, his house and land?"

Mr. Sisk said, "Wait Bonnie, There more to this story. I think it is the main reason Mr. Franks wants Norman to have his property. Maybe your Mom and Dad can tell you more. Let me tell you what he told me."

He took a deep breath thinking before he continued with, "Mr. Frank told me he had married his sweetheart when he was nineteen. After a few years, they had moved here with two kids and one on the way. Built the house you saw and cleared the land while living in a tent. He would raise vegetables and small animals selling them at the Farmers Market around the area. The children eventually moved out and only his wife and he remained. Then one day about twenty years ago awful events happen. One of our attractive rattle snakes struck his wife, Sara, and killed her while she was working in the garden. Sara was the love of his life. It seems that after Sara died, he stopped caring about anything. He just started living from day to day letting everything take care of itself. He had thought of moving to an area near his children many times. But time passed and they are now in their mid-sixes and none of them are interested in his property unless he gives it to them in which he knew they would just sell it. Then he met your parents and watched you grow into a fine young man. When he heard you were looking for a house to buy, he decided instead of letting his children sale it to a stranger he wanted you to have it. As he watched you grew, he saw a lot of himself in you. He knew you would fix the place back up as it once was. So he decided to basically give the place to you at a selling price he knew you could afford. He also told me your children will have the biggest playground in the world and in his eyes the best father also."

Mr. Sisk took a drink of his coffee and as he did I pondered over what he had just told us. I could fix the place up. Grow vegetables like Mr. Franks did and sale them at the Farmer's market. I could afford the two hundred needed to buy the place if I save every penny I make for a while. Then Bonnie and I could get married. The house may need a little work. But, it is nothing compared to have to build a new one. These thoughts were running through my head when Bonnie said, "Daddy, will you help us buy Mr. Franks place."

Mr. Sisk set his coffee cup down and with a smile said, "Wait, and let me tell you something before we go any farther. I have already talked with Normans' parents and for one of our wedding gifts to the love of our lives we have already purchase the property and as of the day you two get married, it's all yours."

"Oh Daddy," Bonnie said as she jumped out of chair and placed her arms around him almost spilling his coffee. Tears were flowing out of her as well as me. I thank God always for bringing him into my life. I could never repay him for his love and instructions while he taught me the car repair trade and his willingness to allow me to marry his daughter. Our tears just flowed.

The wedding was set with Reverend Young at the Calvary Baptist Church two weeks after we signed the papers for Mr. Frank's property. I was ordered to stay out of the wedding preparation which to my thinking was good thing. My only input was choosing the best man. I asked my buddy, Gary, and Bonnie asked his sister, Becky, to be her hand maiden.

On the day of the wedding, the whole community of Guff turned out for it. Tables and chairs were set outside the church and it seemed everybody brought their best dish. Several barbeque pits were smoking as well as boil crabs and shrimp. It was a cool November day.

I could hear many of the ladies thanking God as they entered the church.

I of course was a nervous wreck as I paced around the church yard. I had on my best suit on and everybody that was placing food on the tables would shake my hand or make some wise crack about getting married to the most beautiful girl in town. I just nodded my head and smile. It wasn't that I was getting married that I was nervous. It was the standing before the whole community of Guff that had me pacing. I thought we would have a nice quiet wedding. That went out the window when Mom stood and told everybody in church what was about to happen. They then began to quiz her on what they could bring and such. I decided right then and there it was out of my hands. Of course Bonnie was joyful at having a big wedding.

I kept checking my pocket making sure I had her wedding ring.

Grandpa John and Grandma Eva out of the blue provided us with our wedding rings. I thank them and asked where they got them. Their answer was the rings were promise to you when you were born. Your Great Grandfather gave them to us to give to you if you ever got married. You have his name, Norman Jean Toms. Your Mom and Dad chose to name you after him to honor him.

Dad broke my wondering mine when he hollered from the church door, "It's time to start, Norman."

I then look around and realized I was alone outside the church. I just smiled as I wondered toward Dad. I straighten my suit as I went. When I stood before him I said, "Daddy, I'm a nervous wreck."

Daddy hugged me and said, "Norman, there is nothing to worry about. You are marrying the prettiest girl in state of Texas. You have all of us rejoicing with you. Now you just go in there and meet your future wife. Mom and I want you to know we love you and in our eyes you have turned out to be a very good man. I know you love her and she loves you."

Dad stepped away from the door of the church to let me pass and said, "Now, do you have the vows you want to say to her?" "Yes," I replied.

As I entered the Church, it seems all conversation stopped and everybody looked at me. I've known most of the men and women in the Church all my life. Many were smiling and several stood and shook my hand as I walked toward the front of the Church. I just nodded and thank them. I waved at many who spoke a good word toward me.

As I neared the alter Gary started to walk beside me. We took a few steps and he said, "I think you are the luckiest friend a fellow could ever have. Just look at you, a big wedding and to be marrying the most beautiful girl in the world. You are lucky and I hope and pray I can find a women just like her. I believe it a dream come true."

I place my hand on his shoulder as we walked and said, "Gary, I really thinking God done all the work. I'm just the receiver is all?" Gary stopped as I removed my hand, he said, "What an answer." I position myself on the right side of Reverend Young who said, "Norman, I'm so proud of you. Now do you have the ring and your vows?"

"Yes." I said just before the music began to play, "Come the Bride."

My heart leaped as Bonnie entered wearing a beautiful white flowing wedding that almost touched the floor. Two little girls dressed in yellow and white walked behind her carrying the end of the laced vial that flowed gentle off her off her head and held by a pearl broach which seem to only to enhanced her beauty. In her hand she carried a bouquet of white and yellow flowers outlined in white laced. She was the image of beauty as she carried herself proudly down the aisle toward me. Her smile, her grace, her shoulders back, and her head held high made my heart leap with so much love for her it felt as if she has even touched my sole.

When Bonnie finally positioned herself across from me, the two little girls let go of the lace and raced back toward their parents. The music stopped and I could hear many of the women crying in the background. I did not look to see who. My concentration was on Bonnie and her concentration was upon me. We both were wearing the biggest smile our faces could hold. I took a deep breath and force myself to look at the Reverend Young as he began to speak.

He said, "Folks, most here have known Norman for his entire life. We have watched him grow into a fine young man. Many here have also played with him as he grew. I know he loves the Lord. Now he has found the love of his life. A beautiful girl named Bonnie Sisk. I look at her and I can see she is a beautiful young woman. She carries herself with confidence. I also can see, she loves Norman and he has become the love of her life."

Reverend Young look pass us and into the congregation and with his serious voice said, "Is there anyone here for any reason believed Bonnie and Norman should not be married please speak up now or forever hold your peace."

Reverend Young waited a second, smiled and said, "I can see there is none. In that case, I believe it is time I marry these two lovely people."

Reverend Young took his Bible and held it between us and said,

"Do you have the rings?" Bonnie and I said, "Yes."

Then he said, "I have married couples who want a fast easy wedding. I have married couples that let me do all the talking. As I understand, you two would like to say your vows to each other before we start the proceeding. In that case, Norman would you like to speak first?"

I said, "I would."

Then Reverend Young said, "Begin."

I smiled at Bonnie and said, "Bonnie, I love you with all that within me. I may not be the perfect man in this world and I know I will make mistakes. I vow before you, God and this congregation of friends and family that I will take care of you. I vow that you will never grow hungry or be without cloths are shoes. I vow I will maintain a roof over our heads and a soft bed for us to sleep on. I vow our children will have a good education, well mannered, and respect their peers as well as both of us. But, most important, they will learn to fear God and to believe in our savior, Jesus Christ. I vow to keep you happy and respect your opinion in matters that affect both of us. But the most important vow of all, I will do my upmost to love you and take care of you till the day you or I die."

When I finish, the whole congregation stood and applauded. Reverend Young waited till most were seated again before he turned to Bonnie and said, "Bonnie would you like to say your vows now."

"I would. "Bonnie answered.

"Then proceed." Reverend Young answered.

Bonnie fumbled with the bouquet in her hand a second before she looked at me and with a grin said, "Norman, I love you with all I have within me. I may not be the best women in the world. I vow before you, God and this congregation of friends and family that I will do my best to provide you with a home that will always honor you. I vow I will work with you as you make decisions concerning our welfare. I vow our home will always be clean and I will work side by side with you in whatever you do while providing us and our future children with a decent place to live and play. I vow I will love you in the night and will love you in the day. I vow our children will always be clean and will grow up with good manners. But the most important vow of all, I will do my upmost to love you and take care of you till the day you or I die."

When she had finish, the congregation stood and applauded. Reverend Young waited till most had seat before he wiped the tears from his eyes and said, "Now that your vows are over let us now be married."

Reverend Young turned to me and said, "Norman do you have the ring?"

"I do." I answered as I pulled the ring from my pocket. "Now place your hand on the Bible and repeat after me?"

Reverend Yong said as he places the Bible between us.

I place my hand on the Bible and he said, "Repeat after me."

Waited a second making sure I understood before he began with, "I Norman Toms."

Waited a second as I repeated it before he then said, "with this ring do marry Bonnie Sisk for better or worst so help me God."

I repeated the praised and when I was finish, Reverend Yong removed the Bible and said, "Now please place the ring upon her finger."

I took hold of Bonnie's extended hand and with the biggest smile I could muster place my Great Grandmother's ring upon her finger. Held her hand a second as I look her in the face and for some reason I bent down and kissed her hand before I let go of it.

Reverend Young as he put the Bible between us again said,

"Bonnie do you have his ring?" Bonnie answered, "I do."

Reverend Young said, "Place your hand on the bible and repeat after me."

Bonnie place her hand on the bible and I guess I must have had biggest smile on my face as Reverend Young said, "I, Bonnie Sisk with this ring do marry Norman Toms for better are worst so help me God."

Bonnie repeated the praised and when she had Finish, Reverend

Young quickly removed the Bible and said, "Now please place the ring upon his finger."

I held out my hand which Bonnie took and slowly placed my Great

Grandfather's ring upon my finger.

Reverend Young said, "Now you two kiss before us all."

Bonnie and I both stepped forward and when we met we kissed. It was not a one that just said, "*I love you* kind of kisses." But, a mouthwatering tong touching mouth wide open kiss that lasted till the congregation began to holler and clap. When we let go of each other Reverend Young yell over the clapping and hollering, "Everybody, I would like to present to the Guff community Mr. And Mrs. Toms.

As we slowly walked together down the aisle, many stopped us and shook our hands wishing us a good life and many children. I could see Mom had been crying as well as Dad who stepped before us and said, "I cannot be more proud of happy for you then I am right now. Mother and I want both of you to know we will always be there for you."

Mother stood and hugged Bonnie and said, "I just love you every sense Norman first introduce you."

Bonnie hugged her back and said, "Mom, I love you to and I assure you I will take you care of your son."

Daddy said, "Let them go, Mom. We can talk later outside."

Mr. Sisk was blocking the doorway leading outside and handed me the keys to our house when we stopped before him. He hugged his daughter, smiled at me before he shook my hand and said, "I've not lost a daughter but have gain a son-in-law.

"Daddy," Bonnie said, "Everybody waiting to enjoy the feast that is outside and I think we are standing in their way."

"Let them wait." Mr. Sisk said, "I've lost a daughter to this strange character here beside you and I want to enjoy her company before he drags you off and I may never see you again."

"Daddy, you know that's not true?" Bonnie replied as she hugged her dad again and he yelled, "Let the feast begin."

Six
C H A P T E R

Norman helped Bonnie to seat into the wheelchair clearing his head of the day they were married. Slowly he pushed her into the dining room and positions her beside the kitchen table. Bonnie smiled at him as he placed a cup of lukewarm coffee before her. She took a sipped of it. Her hand shook as she replaced the coffee cup back upon the table and stared out the kitchen window toward the chicken yard where several chickens were busy scratching the ground.

As Norman began to fix their breakfast, he said, "Clara will be here shortly to take you to the doctor. Would you like to listen to the radio?"

There was no response.

Norman left the cooking bacon and turned the radio on. The kitchen filled with a gospel song about the love of

Jesus. As Norman returned back to the bacon, he slowly regained his composure and took a deep breath. It was not what Bonnie did that bothered him it was her enter stillness that sometimes almost cause him to throw up his hands and quit. Sometimes when he felt this way, Norman would go for long walks or stand and watch the chickens scratched. They were such peaceful animals to have around which always calmed him down. But as he watched the chickens scratch, God was always reminded him of his vow he made before him when him and Bonnie were married.

Norman finishes cooking the eggs and bacon and placed the plates upon the kitchen table and sat down beside Bonnie. As was his habit now, he would feed Bonnie a bit and as she chewed, he would take a bit himself or two or three. Norman always finished his plate first and waiting patiently for Bonnie to finish. Then clean the plates and place them in the dishwasher.

Bonnie continued to stare out the window and as Norman looked at her he said under his breath, "I wonder what she thinking or is she thinking at all. The doctors said she really asleep with her eyes open. I wonder sometimes."

Norman shook his head trying to clear his mind of the negative thoughts that often filled it after Bonnie became real sick. Turning away from the kitchen counter, Norman exited out of the house onto the back porch. The summer heat hit him as he exited the house. Norman looked up toward the shy, lifted his hands into the air and said, "Lord please keep giving me the strength to continue. I love you for giving Bonnie to me for such a long and beautiful life. Please keep us safe while we take her to see the doctor. I also ask that you keep my heart joyful as you return to me memories of the past that Bonnie and I had together. Help me always to have a smile upon my face as I help my loving wife in the last days of her life. I will always thank you for her. I love her dearly. Bonnie has always been my joy in the morning. She has been the center of our household. She gave birth to our fine children. She has taken care of me and our children during our good times as well as the bad. I will always give you praise and honor no matter what happens in our last days. For without you to hold my hand, I would have wonder and strayed far from the fold. For without you, we have no hope for tomorrow."

Norman bowed his head and spoke a few words in tongs,

"Masahna Kee Lama Lasanlama Kama."

Norman lowered his arms and looked out over his property. Sam wondered over to him just wagging his tail wanting to be petted. Then Norman noticed Superman meowing upon the railing with eyes open as wide as they get, Norman smile as he asked, "I guess you two want to be fed. Am I right?"

Sam barked as if saying yes just before he spun around all excited. Superman continued to meow from the railing. Norman turned and as he entered back into the house

Superman quickly followed still meowing. Norman filled superman's bowl and took Sam a cup full with several doggie bones. As they ate, Norman wonder toward the chicken yard where the chickens were beginning to fuss and run back and forth anxious for him to feed them. When he entered the yard, the chickens gathered around his feet and fluttered themselves. He opens the feed barrel, scooped a can full of feed and cast it across the yard. The chickens scattered after it. Norman checked the nests and gathered six eggs from them.

When Norman exited the chicken yard, he stopped and looked out over his property. The house could use a coat of paint and only three pecans trees still stood around it. Two were destroyed by Hurricane Fred and one just plain died. The garden area appeared to be growing fine. Norman glanced down the fence line and the zucchini had just reach the top of the fence and he could see several of the zucchini hanging among the leaves. Norman walked over and pulled any he thought were long enough to harvest. He wondered back to the porch, set the zucchini down, grabbed a basket and headed for the garden with Sam in toe. He checked all the plants and when he left he had three yellow squash, one white squash, five cucumbers and several tomatoes that were almost ripe.

Norman bend and checked how the water melons and kasha were growing and was please to fine that there was now a number of fruit among the large leaves. When he straightens back upped, he glances out into the pasture where several oil well pumps were going round and round. Norman smiled for they sure have provided him with a full bank account. They had been pumping for almost forty years. Ever sense they discovered oil under his property many years ago.

Norman thought as he made his way back toward the house, "Yea that was almost ten years after we moved into the house. I had made enough by then, to buy forty more acres from old man Wilson after he became sick with cancer to help him pay his doctor bills. I took a loan out from the bank to buy it. Then two years later paid it off after the first oil check came in. As I look back, I have been blessed by God that is for sure. But, we first moved in was not easy. The house needed a lot of work. I remember the first day I move in."

It was a week after we were married. As a marriage gift, Bonnie and I were giving an all paid week in Galveston to enjoy the food and ride the rides at Play land Park. We even went deep sea fishing one day. While we were there, Mom, Dad and Mr. Sisk cleaned our house from front to back. Mowed the yard and Mr. Sisk repaired the old truck. It smoked but ran.

When Bonnie and I returned, I carried her into the house and we just laughed. We were all alone and were shock to find out how spotless the place was when we entered. My bed suit from the Mom's and Dad's house was setup in the bedroom. There were new towels in the bathroom and when Bonnie checked the kitchen she found her Mom's set of dishes arrange in the cabinets. Bonnie just sat down on the floor and cried that her Dad would give her such a precious gift.

I could tell Mom and Dad had clean the rest of the house. Still it needed a lot of repair. We took our first bath and that night we rejoiced over our new house with love making.

I began repairing the house after work and on the weekends. Mr. Sisk and Dad also helped and both seem to know how to do everything. My respect for them grew as they helped me repair the plaster which was gone from beneath the windows throughout the house. They knew just how to repair it after I repaired the windows with new wood and caulking.

Leveling the house was done in one day. We use several jacks and cement blocks. But, the painting was left to Bonnie and me.

Bonnie and Mom just love to prepare meals in the spotless kitchen while we men were fixing this or that. It wasn't too long the house was looking fairly decent in Bonnie eyes. I then began to repair the chicken yard. When I was sure it would hold chickens, I checked around and Mr. Ward gave us ten laying hens and one old rooster.

The tractor was another thing. It had been sitting so long, that to me it appeared a hopeless case. Mr. Sisk thought otherwise. He said, "It just like an old car that has not been running for years. We'll put some oil in each cylinder, get new spark plugs and soak the carburetor in gas. After a few days we'll see if we can get it to turn over. If so, then it is only matter of reattaching everything and cranked her. She'll run you'll see."

Sure enough it worked. I had to hand cranked the motor many times before I got it started. It needed a better muffler and better tires. Mr. Sisk said, "Used it anyway."

Which I did and it was not long a nice garden spot was plowed upped and planted. It was late in the season to start. Still, I thought we could get a few vegetables this year. I also worked and got the mower working and was soon mowing the pasture after work and on the weekends. I went slow and easy hoping the darn thing would keep running.

Mending the fences took money and Bonnie and I did not have a whole lot of. So, I budget our finances and was soon fending the fence around our property. By this time, I was really enjoying married life.

Going to bed every night with a Bonnie lying beside me was not only comforting it was pleasurable also. Our love making and exploring each other's body was a joy for both of us. I learned what she enjoyed and she learned what I liked.

Then one-week end while I was sitting down on the pouch taking a break from repairing the fence near the house, Bonnie came out on the pouch with a glass of ice tea for me. As I took the glass from her, Bonnie said, "Norman, I think I'm pregnant."

My mouth fell open and my mine went blank as I grasped just what Bonnie just said. I calmly set the glass upon the table, stood and I said, "Are you sure?"

"Yes I am." Bonnie answered. "This is the second month I have miss my period and lately I have been feeling kind of strange. I called your Mom and we had a good talk. We both agree that I am pregnant."

My heart was just rejoicing with the news Bonnie just told me and I could not control myself as I began to shout and dance around the pouch. Bonnie just stood with her head twisted upon her left shoulder like she always did when she thought I was too excited or making a fool out of myself.

I stopped my dancing and said, "I hope it a boy."

Bonnie just smile and said, "That is for God to determine. I think it will be a girl myself."

My heart was still rejoicing and I controlled myself from shouting and asked her, "Do I need to do anything? Like help you are something?"

"Nope," Bonnie answered. "The baby should not affect me until I'm eight or nine months into my pregnancy. I will continue to work at the dinner and work around here also. Just because I'm pregnant does not mean that I'm helpless."

"I was just thinking of the baby is all?" I answered.

Bonnie started to reenter the house and as she did she said, "I'll be just fine. I just hope I don't get fat."

"Wait," I said, "Does that mean we can't make love anymore?"

Bonnie turned and gave me a glassy eye look, smiled at me and said, "Not for a while."

"Whew," I answered as I let out a deep breath I was holding just as Bonnie disappeared into the house.

I returned to my seat on the porch and took a drink of the cold tea Bonnie had brought me. A smiled filled my face as I thought of what a baby would bring into our lives. I bet Mom right now is telling everybody in town the good news. I guess I better get one of the rooms ready. Paint it with bright cheerful colors and make it baby proof. We have to buy diapers and baby bottles along with Toys. Suddenly, my concentration was interrupted when Bonnie yelled from the kitchen lunch was ready.

When I stood to enter the kitchen, I suddenly remembered what happened few weeks ago when Beth actually seduce me saying after our love that night she would become pregnant. I just could not help myself as I jumped into the air and side kicked my shoes together in happiness.

Seven
C H A P T E R

*W*hen Norman returned back to the house, Norman place the vegetables in the basket beside the door and took a glance back inside the house making sure Bonnie was still sitting beside the window and found her still staring out the window just as he left her. He returned to the porch and walk around to the front of the house. Unwrapped the water hose and began spraying Bonnie's brightly colorful flowers that was blooming along the front of the house. Norman continued around the edge of the house and when he was satisfied all was well watered. He rounds the water hose back upped.

He returned to the back pouch with a water can in toe and began watering the potted plants around the pouch. When Norman was finish he reentered the house and notice Bonnie was still staring out the window. As he walked over to her, Norman grabbed a towel and gentle wiped the droll located around the edge of her month. Bonnie look upped at him and smiled.

"Clara will be here any minute now." Norman said as he sat down beside her. He examines Bonnie's coffee and saw she had not touched it. Stood and placed it beside the sink and poured another cup full. Then just as Norman sat down beside Bonnie, he heard Clara's car pull into the driveway. Then he heard Clara yelling at Freddy saying, "Leave the dog alone. You'll get dirty and we are going into town."

"All I wanted to do is pet him is all." Freddy answered.

"That better be all your doing." Clara said as she stepped onto the pouch. "Last time we were here; it took an hour to get all the dirt off you."

"I'll be good." Freddy said as he took off running with Sam in toe. As Clara entered the kitchen she said, "I give up. If he gets dirty this time, he stays dirty."

"Hello Clara." Norman said as he stood and gave her a big I love you hug.

Clara responded by returning the hug and as they parted she asked, "How Mom this morning?"

"She is about the same." Norman answered. "I got her ready to go."

As Clara hugged Bonnie she said, "I hope this Doctor's visit he give us something that will help her."

"I think they are doing all that they can." Norman said as he sat back down and took a sip of his coffee.

As Clara sat down beside Bonnie, Norman said, "I got some coffee made. Do you want some?"

"Not really." Clara answered. "I think I'm coffee out. Had three cups already and Freddy been running me ragged?"

"Not your precious grandson. He would never do that." Norman said with a laugh.

"I guess not." Clara answered. "But sometime I think he tries me a little."

Clara began trying to bring up a conversation with Bonnie. Bonnie just smiled at her as if she understood Clara's concern over her. Clara looked over at Norman and he could see the sadness in her face from the lack of response Bonnie gave her.

Clara said, "She getting worst isn't she, Dad." "Yes," I answered.

Clara stood and walked behind the wheelchair and said, "I guess we better get going. I hope Freddy is still clean?"

"He'll be alright." Norman said as he held the door open for Clara to push Bonnie out of the house and onto the pouch.

"Let's go, Freddy." Clara yelled as she pushed the wheelchair down the ramp Norman had built for Bonnie after it was apparent she was not well and headed toward the car.

As Clara position the wheelchair for Bonnie to enter the car, Freddy came running upped to the car just a panting followed closely by Sam whose tail was just a wagging.

Freddy said, "Hello, Grandma."

Suddenly, Bonnie smiled and said, "Well Hello, Oh are we going somewhere."

"Sure are, Grandma." Freddy answered, "Can I sit beside you?" "You sure can," Bonnie said as she lifted herself from off the wheelchair and entered the car.

Freddy quickly ran to the other side and entered the car and took a seat beside his Grandma.

Clara and Norman did not say a word as they took the front seats for Freddy must had awaking Bonnie from her awful staring state. They just look at each other and knew each other's thoughts.

Clara fasten her seatbelt and she said, "Freddy, help Grandma with her seatbelt now."

"Ok," Freddy answered as he reached for the seatbelt beside him and pulled it across Bonnie.

Bonnie just smiled as he locked the two ends together.

Clara back the car onto the street and it was not long they were on the freeway headed for the downtown area where the Hope Center was located. Only Freddy rambling broke the stillness.

Norman sat watching the country side and ad signs until a sign appeared showing a Marine with the catchphrase, "Be all you can be. Join the Marines."

Norman thought, "I wasn't a Marine but I did get drafted alone with Tom Sneed during the Korea War. Too bad he was killed."

Norman thought, "I got him to join me in learning to repair trucks and tanks after we finish basic training. If I remember right, at signup we told a tall tell that he worked for Mr. Sisk allowing him to join with me. Mr. Sisk seemed to have had something to do with me getting into the mechanic section of the service and I thought might as well get someone I knew to go with me. We had a lot of fun to. We stuck together like glue and I just laugh at his attempt to catch a date with one of the girls."

Norman look back down the road and under his breath said, "I sure was young back then. I think I was always covered with grease working at the 512TH Ordnance group in Korea with Tom Sneed as my partner."

Norman settled into his car seat and thought of the day Sneed died. "I sure like him. I got him to follow me into the mechanic area of the army thinking we could work together after we got out. Mr. Sisk had something to do with it I believed as we stood by the Captain's office after basic training both of us were assigned to the mechanic school to learn diesel engine repair that was used in the many type of military tanks. There was the M4 Sherman, M26 Pershing, M46 Patton, M26 Chaffee and my favorite, the M41Centurion. We always called them by their number. They sure did break down a lot and it seemed always on the battle field and had to be toed in by the old Diamond T Transport to our repair shop. If I remember right, there were over 100 Tank battles during the war.

I never forgot how Tom would look at the engine that had been hit by the North Koreans and always say, "Let's get this baby back up and lets these guys get revenge."

But those that came in really destroyed, I always wondered what the guys inside were thinking when a big shell hit them and if any survived. I admired those guys greatly looking at the damage tanks. Tom and I fix them as best we could and off to the front they went. There was times when we had to travel with the Diamond T and help load a destroyed tank, especially if Tom and I got ourselves in trouble with Captain Klenz. I think it was mostly when Tom got drunk and didn't show up for his shift till noon. I tried to cover for him but it did not work always.

We were working on one of the new M46's that had lost it oil plug and ended upped turning a rod. It belonged to one of the tank commanders and Captain Klenz wanted it to be out of the shop quickly.

Captain Klenz stopped by and asked, "Where is Sneed, Toms?" "He is getting parts." I would answer every time I lifted my head from beneath the engine of the M46."

"Well, tell him I would like to see him in my office when he comes in and that includes you." Captain Klenz said with his command voice.

"Yes Sir." I replied.

I was just replacing the oil pan when Sneed showed. He still was very red eyed and had a face that could not be anything but a hangover looks. He sat down beside me and asked, "Were you able to cover for me?"

"Nope," I answered as I was tightening the last pan nut.

As he rolled back onto the ground Seed said, "Darn, I am trouble now?"

"Not only you?" I answered as I crawl out from beneath the M26 with its Ford engine.

"Sorry, I really did not desire this to happen." Sneed said. "Those darn sailors at the poker game did this to me. They made me drink that darn native drink during the poker game. You know the one they called, "Fill bad in the morning."

As I stood, I said, "I stay away from that stuff. Anyway, let me fill this baby up with oil and while I'm doing that, why don't you just climb in her and let us see if she'll start."

Sneed stood and moved away from the rear and seem to struggle a little as he climbed upped to the hatch and entered. I watched and smiled as he disappeared down the hatch. I never try to start one. That was Sneed's job. He seems to know just how to apply the diesel and work the glow plug where the darn engines start every time.

This time was no different as I listen to the roar of the engine. I adjusted the timing to the perfect pitch I have learned when an engine was in impeccable time. When I slam the rear cover down, Sneed cut the engine knowing all is well.

After Sneed exited the M26, we clean the work area and after about an hour Sneed climbed back into the tank and drove it out of the work area. I followed watching the operation of the M26 making sure all was well with her drive system and tracks. Sneed parked her in line with the other Pershing Tanks. There must have been close to forty of them in the lot and within military requirements with all the tanks parked by typed of tank so many feet apart and in perfect alignment.

As Sneed, with my guidance, parked the M26 among the many other M26's I looked across the parking zone at the many different tanks and thought, "It wasn't too long ago it was not this. The war was winding down with all the peace talks and many of the crews have gone home and it appears they are not being replaced. I've worked on all the different tanks and I like the big heavy M46. I always thought with its big guns it just looked mean. Most of the tanks were the Sherman we call the Easy Eight and the light M24 which I light to work on also. There off to the far right were even some of the British M41 Centurions with its Rolls Royce twelve-cylinder engine.

We stopped at the dispatched and reported all was well with the Commander's Tank when we heard behind us coming from Captain Klenz office, "Toms, Sneed, in here right now."

We turn toward the Captain and I said, "Captain, is it alright if we clean up a bit. Both of us got crud all over us and need to wash up first."

"Ok," Captain Klenz said as he turned to reenter his office he added, "Don't be too long?"

We washed and wasn't long both of us stood before him. He had paper work scattered in some kind of organized way across his desk. Look us over before concentrating upon Sneed he said, "Sneed, I should get mad for being late this time but I'm not. I saw you and those sailors last night. I saw hold your own by walking out of the club while they on the other hand they could not. Quit empress."

Sneed was now fingering his cap said, "Thank you Captain Klenz."

Captain Klenz stood and pointed toward his map and as he did he said, "Now boys, I have a problem on that map. I was going to share it with all the teams in the shop but there a big battle going on over at Pork Chop Hill right now. My problem is two teams on the Lighting T have been rotated out and the replacements have not arrived. That where you two come in. I know you two have licenses to drive the Lighting T. I already have Cash and Leor's Lighting T out picking up a M26 and need two divers to go pick up a badly damage tank. Now I need you two to go to the 17th Artillery and pick up a M26. It is located near Pork chop Hill."

"You want us to go all alone just the two of us?" I asked.

"You'll have the normal escort with you." Captain Klenz answered before he gave a small laugh.

Sneed said, "That means we are on our own."

Captain Klenz sat back down and said, "I choose you two for you have both taken many trips on the Lighting T and know the procedure to collect the broken down tanks."

"I believe we do." I answered.

Sneed feeling his fore head with a tired looked asked, "When do we have to leave."

"I should send you out now." Captain Klenz said, "But, I reported to them we will pick it upped tomorrow. Besides, I do not send any of my solders out in the night. You'll leave early in the morning."

Sneed said, "Can we rest till then?

Captain Klenz lean back in his chair and said, "From the look of you, I believe you do. Now this will be a dangerous pick upped tomorrow. There a big battle going on there and lots of artillery. It is one of the M26 tanks used to protect and travel with 17TH artillery and guard them. From what I understand, it is sitting in middle of the road or something."

"Captain Klenz, where is this Pork Chop Hill?" I asked.

Captain Klenz stood and walked over to the large map on the wall and pointed to an area near the front lines about twenty-five miles from here and he said, "You going have to asked exactly where the M26 is unless you come across it in the road. That is all I have for you right now."

He returned to his seat while Sneed and I examine the area indicated to us by the Captain. It was right in the middle of the Korean hills. I follow the path we would have to take before turning to the Captain and asked, "Why are we picking the M26 upped in the middle of the battle? Don't we usually wait?"

Captain Klenz said, "I don't know I was just ordered to. I think it is because it is blocking the road are an area they need to place their guns."

Next day we climbed into the Diamond T and left the compound heading north. The roads were so crowed by Koreans families heading south away from the fighting. There many trucks and other types of military equipment. It made the path northward slow. As they near the front, there were no more Koreans and their carts and other types of travel allowing us to travel a lot faster with other loaded duce and halves. Soon we heard the sound of the battle. By now I was began fingering my M1 watching the country side closely for any sign of the enemy.

There were several companies of solders marching north and we often pass an ambulance heading south and even passing us as they returned. The sound of the booming artillery was growing closer and at times they could see the explosions from the Chinese artillery across the hilly surface.

I began to pray under my breath, "Let not one hit our Lighting T and the road." I kept repeating the prayer as we drew closer and closer to the artillery. We topped a small rise and there flat in the middle of the road sat the M26. Where it sat was causing the duce and halves that were loaded with artillery shells to go drive around it. I could see right off it had been hit hard by one of the Chinese artillery. Sneed quickly turned the Lighting T and I guided him into position to load her. I release the pull cable and taken hold of the end I pulled it along as I crawl beneath the M26 to hook it.

Sneed climb down from the Cab and stood at the pulley controls waiting for me to crawl out from beneath M26. I started to back up when the first of many Chinese artillery shells exploded around us. I was rocked back and forth from them. I quite in shocked as I slowly drug myself from beneath and as I tried to stand my blurred vision cleared and I was Sneed all slumped onto the ground. I stagger to him and saw right off he was dead. I really began to weep as sat down beside him, reached and held his lifeless body in my arms crying out to God for my friend. I'll never forget that moment as long as I live. The moment I bent down to touch his shattered body to only to see the face of the dead friend.

Eight
CHAPTER

*N*orman was still pondering over Sneed when Clara pulled into the doctors' office parking lot. There were several cars parked within located at the owner's desire. When Norman turned to see if Bonnie was able to leave the car and saw right off she was not for she had returned back to her staring state. Freddy did not notice for he was trying to open the car door before Clara had unlocked it. Norman could tell Freddy in away was very concern about his Grandma. He kept looking at her and was overjoyed when the door opened. As he exited he turned and pulled on Bonnie's arm saying, "Come on Grandma we are here at the doctor."

Bonnie yield to his pulling and by the time Normal had exited she was standing by the car being led by Freddy who had not let go of her arm. He walked her slowly into the

Doctor's Office followed by Clara and Norman. Freddy led her to a seat. Clara took a seat beside her. Norman reported in and afterwards sat down beside Clara. As he did Norman said, "Now we wait."

Freddy kept everyone entertain till a nurse stuck her head out the door and said, "Hello Norman, why don't you bring Bonnie on end,"

Norman stood and just as Freddy did he took Bonnie's arm and lightly pulled on it raising her from her seat. Normal led her through the door and as they entered Nurse Sandy pointed to a wheelchair and said, "Please place her in it. I personally don't understand why you don't move her in one? It would be a lot easier on you?"

Norman as he placed her leads upon the foot rest he said, "Give her as much of a normal life as I can. Placing Bonnie in one would be like sentencing her to death. You can understand that can't you?"

Nurse Sandy as she started to move Bonnie she answered, "That I can. I surely can. I've seen them in wheelchairs everyday and most of them have this look you see when someone rather be doing anything but sitting in a in a wheelchair at a Doctor's Office."

Nurse Sandy pushed Bonnie into one of the examining rooms. There was talk between them how Bonnie was doing as Nurse Sandy checked her vital signs and pulled several vials of blood. Smile and left the room.

Norman found a seat and waited. It wasn't long till

Doctor Estes entered. He asked several questions and after a few minutes of examination he said, "I checked the blood examination before I came in and it appears her body is shutting down. I've done all I can do for her and from our experience when the blood indicates shut down it means she could leave us at anytime. I just hate to tell any spouse her or his love one is near death."

Normal from his seat said, "I've been expecting it anytime."

Doctor Estes continue to examine Bonnie and said, "It could be tonight or several years from now. If you are not ready, I believe you should."

"We prepare for this many years ago." Norman said, "In fact, it has been so long I do not know if they will remember me."

They continued to discuss Bonnie behavior and Norman realized from Doctor Estes he would soon have to put her in nursing home where she could be watched twenty four hours a day. Norman thanked Doctor Estes for all the years he has helped Bonnie and wheeled Bonnie out into the waiting room. Left her with Clara and returned to the office window and received the bill which he paid.

As Clara drove them home Normal described what Doctor Estes told him what he needed to do by placing Bonnie in a Nursing Home. Clara did not like the idea and she just knew the other children would not like it either.

Norman could see tears in her eyes when he said, "Clara,

your mother going to need a lot more care than I can give her."

"I don't like it." Clara said as she glance back at Bonnie and saw her only sitting there staring with no emotion on her face.

"Your Mother is about to die and nothing neither of us can do about it," Norman said sadly.

"I know," Clara answered.

Norman turned and reached over the seat and took hold of Bonnie's hand and with a smile said, "She been the apple of my eye ever sense we met and we were so young. We had our ups and downs and our life was filled with love and children. Great friends that have come and gone and the best experience for both of us was when God filled us with his Holy Spirit. I know we both have done things wrong and we have not displayed love towards other as we should have."

Turning toward Clara he said, "Clara, when your Mother and I began to notice she had a problem remembering things, she and I had had long talked. Our discussion centered on the gift of God and his promises he gave us. Thus, just because she will be leaving us soon, I know without a doubt I will meet her in heaven after I too am laid to rest. I know I also am not long for this world either."

Clara said, "Stopped that? I do not want to hear something that will happen tomorrow. Today is today and you need to hear your own words. You remember. I bet you told us this, thousands of times. When you told us that today was a new day. One you have never seen and when it is over never see again. Thus, what are you going to do to remember it by?"

Norman sat quiet thinking on her words as Clara pulled into the driveway. When she had placed car into park she looked at her dad and gently said, "Remember what you told us. I learn to live that way and I believe provided my life with many adventures and excitements as I made so many wrong decisions. I taught your grandchildren to live that way and even I know they told their children the same."

Freddy interrupted their conversation as he opened the door and said, "Come on Grandma your home now."

He took hold of her hand and gently pulled. Bonnie followed him and stood outside of the car. Gently he led her toward the front door. Norman quickly exited the car and said, "Let me open the door first before you walk her onto the porch."

It was not long, Bonnie was sitting in her favorite chair and Normal began fixing the last two cups in the coffee pot for Clara and him. All conversation concerning Bonnie soon changed to Freddy and Clara's need to return home, said their goodbyes and Clara with a refill of coffee in her hand, they left.

Norman stood on the porch watching them leave with Freddy waving like crazy at him as they drove away. He smiled and waved back till they were out of sight. He stood still awhile upon the porch thinking, "She been the apple of our eye for she was an extra. Judy was going on twelve when she came along. Bonnie and I chose just to have three children and me and my ways always exciter her enough for us to have great sex at night. The outcome was Clara who was born into a house full of love. Her sister and brother they sure did love her and I know they taught her many bad habits when she was a child for she would copy them sometimes to the letter. Those were days full of life. Getting them up in the morning and off to school was always to me a hassle. They seem to fight us and I really do not blame them." Norman was still pondering over the children's early life when he entered back into the house. Bonnie still had not moved as if she was here yet living in another world also. "Shoot," Norman thought. "She could be sitting there talking to Angles around us right now."

Norman drew closer to Bonnie's ears and said, "Bonnie, tell them I love them also and I can't wait to see them as you do."

As Norman straightens himself to a standing position, he could see, just ever so lightly, a smile was upon her lips. The lips he has kissed a million times. Love was always upon them as everyday day they made sure to kiss each other and their kids. He thought, "I guessed our love was a kiss getting ready to happen and we diffidently love to kiss. Gee, I miss that. Now I feel such kissing will never happen again until I meet her again on the street of gold."

Norman moved his vision to her beautiful blue eyes that has looked upon him all their life together with love he never took for granted but always returned it double if he could. How she those beautiful blue eyes bring out the good in everybody. She was the heart of their church and seemed to work miracles as she organized events there. Everybody loved her and I know there were many look forward for that love her as she knocked at their door and there was some that didn't because she always was coming to get them to do something, either at the church or for some stranger or for one of the members of the church.

Norman returned to the kitchen and began fixing a new pot of coffee. As he pulled the pot from beneath the drip area he thought, "Bonnie sure got herself in trouble several times and I had to bail her out with a few dollars. But she and Billy Joe was another thing. She would get so upset with him and yet love him the most in the church. I think if Billy Joe was still alive and should so happen to walk into her kitchen and say hi, she would instantly come out of the state she in and tell him that she loved him even though sometimes he would make her so mad she just wanted to scream at him."

Norman filled the coffee pot with hot water and smile to himself as he filled the small holding tank on the coffee maker.

"She was a pistol back then that was for sure." he thought as he turned the maker on. Then he gave Bonnie a respectful look, just before he left the kitchen and sat down in his lazyboy recliner across from her. He thought about picking his guitar up but his thoughts returned back to Billy Joe. Norman remembered he was one of the elders of the church and did not like my sweet Bonnie interfering in everybody's lives especially his.

Norman thought, "I believed it was about Christmas time when it happened. The children by this time had all gotten married with kids and Bonnie was determined to make sure everyone at the House of Prayer had a wonderful Christmas and to her, Billy Joe was no different even though he was always given her hints for her to leave him alone."

Bonnie would always greet him at church with, "Good morning Billy Joe. How have you been doing?" Just before she would give him a big hugged which he always seems to reject. Bonnie notice but she was bound and determined to not let that get under her skin.

She would say, "Now Billy Joe. You know a hug a day keeps the doctor away?"

He always returned, "Yea, as far away from you as possible."

I think it was two weeks before Christmas time and Billy Joe came up with a plan so devious, I even today admired what he did. I think was just after church that it started.

Bonnie was asking everyone as they exited the church if she or he needed any help over Christmas holidays like wrap presents, cook a meal or special dish. I guess Billy Joe the moment he heard her requests must have smile deeply within himself as he stood before her and smiling he said, "Bonnie I do have a need and I would be so delighted if you would come to my house and help me fix a couple dishes for my family that would be visited me on Christmas Eve. I never had a Christmas meal for them before except for a pizza or fried chicken."

"Why Billy Joe, I would love to help you." Bonnie answered.

Still smiling he said, "Stop by house on the morning of Christmas Eve. The back door will be open for it leads into the kitchen. On the kitchen table I'll have a list I need you to fix and all the ingredients to make them."

"Oh Billy Joe I make you and your family the best side dishes you ever tasted." Bonnie exclaimed.

"You promise you will fix everything on my list?" Billy Joe said and that smile was still on his face.

"I sure do." Bonnie answered. "Right here before everyone and God I promise I will fix everything on your list."

Billy held out his hand and Bonnie shook it being so happy to help Billy Joe whom she really liked. I was standing to the side and looking at Billy Joe I knew he was up to something for this was way out of his character and that sneaky smile on his face, I knew Bonnie got herself in trouble and she diffidently did not know she was and I for one was not going to tell her.

Bonnie was so excited over fixing Billy Joe's meal she made a nice apple to leave with them. Then the Sunday just a few days before Christmas, again Billy Joe confronted her as the end of service with the same sneaky smile.

As he hugged Billy Joe, Bonnie said, "I promise I would be there didn't I? Whatever you have for me I would fix it, I promise."

Billy Joe still had that smile on his fast as he left her and exited out the doors. Bonnie was full of joy being asked by Billy Joe to do anything and to her it was a great honor for all she ever got from before him was to rejection.

That Tuesday morning, I drove her to Billy Joe's house. I parked the car in front and we walked around to the back door. I notice his car was gone and as we neared the back door I said, "Bonnie, I don't think Billy Joe is here? I don't see his car anywhere."

"It is alright," Bonnie answered as she reached for the back door knob. "He already told me he would not be here and to go right on end."

When entered the kitchen was a mess. Dirty dishes stack around the sink. All the pots and pans were also dirty and I could hear Bonnie under her breath saying, "That so and so has done it to me this time. He thinks I would just walk out and throw up my hands and say no way. I'll show him."

I started to leave when she grabbed my arm and said, "Where do you think you are going? I put my word down and I be darn if he going to get this over me."

"But Bonnie, I did not volunteer?" I laughed. "You did."

Not letting go of my arm she pulled me back into the kitchen and placed me at the sink with dirty dishes and said, "Get busy. If he wants special supper, he's going to get one with cleaned dishes."

I just shrug my shoulders, took a deep breath and began organizing the dishes to wash. Afterward, I search for dry towels and found a nice storage area beside the icebox full of them.

Bonnie had cleared the large dining table and set what was on it arrange upon the nice stained china cabinet. She opened it and instantly found a really nice table cover. In no time she had the large dining table covered and set with Billy Joe's finest dishes. When she returned to the kitchen, she cleared the breakfast table and set the dishes before me.

It took me an hour to wash, dry and put away all the dishes and as I cleaned the pots I handed her the ones she wanted. By noon the Turkey stuff with sausage dressing along with the Ham was cooking each based in her own favorite sauces she liked to use. The smell was making me hungry so I left the table and said, "Think I'll go get us a burger or chicken sandwich. What do you want to drink?"

"Nothing," Bonnie answered as she was preparing the sweet potatoes to cook.

I left and after fifteen minutes returned with our food. Bonnie was sitting at the table waiting on me and as I entered the kitchen she said,

"Got everything on and cooking."

I sat the food on the table and said, "I think he got you this time. Here you are fixing his family a big meal and he not even here to help you."

Bonnie looked at me and I saw a big smile come over her face as she said, "He did not. I was thinking he did when I first entered his house. But as I cook, the Lord reviled to me I was not getting over by Mr. Billy Joe in cooking and cleaning his kitchen and dining room. He indeed needed our help to prepare a fancy meal that just could be his last one he will ever have with his children."

"What you talking about?" I asked as sat down across from her and started to pull two chicken sandwiches from the bag I had placed on the table.

As I sat her sandwich before Bonnie she said, "Don't you see? Billy Joe really needed our help and was just too ashamed to ask directly for it. It is so clear to me now."

"Well still a little foggy for me." I answered as I opened my sandwich.

Bonnie picked her sandwich off the table and while she opened it.

"You might not understand but I do. When they come

in later today, they will find I have fixed the best Christmas meal ever for him and his children. He said they will be here at six so we must be gone and the table ready by fifteen till."

I helped where I was needed and exactly at Five forty-five we left. The table was set and covered with the finest Turkey and dressing, ham, sweet potatoes, mash potatoes, corn, peas, cranberry sauce, white gravy and sweet bread rolls. Three pies set on the kitchen counter with plates ready to serve with vanilla ice cream waiting in the freezer.

We never knew the outcome of the meal Bonnie created only that from then on, Billy Joe came to Bonnie for a hug and never again made a wise crack about her cooking but would only say, "She is the best."

Nine
CHAPTER

*W*ithin a month after seeing the doctor Norman started to notice signs of weakness in Bonnie's body that were not apparent before. He loved her so and here she was, slowly disappearing before his eyes. She and him would love to hold hands and now her hand only sits empty of any feeling if he should reach and take her hand in his. It was just limp flesh with fingers resting in his strong hand. Norman could see that thou she lives she really was actually dead for her body has yet to give up.

Norman would fix coffee in the morning and after he had place Bonnie in her chair. He would sit and talk to her as if she could hear and understand very word he spoke. He would talk about the weather or what he was going to fix for lunch and supper. He covered the children of what he knew of their lives. But most of the time he drifted into their past and talk of the good times they had together. Sometimes he would wonder off into some bad times like the time her Father died.

Norman had just finish telling Bonnie what they were having for lunch when for some unknown reason he began to think about her Dad. He took a drink of his warm coffee and said, "Bonnie, did you know your father gave us the life we now have. He was such a good man and I know he loved you for he made sure your hubby was someone he liked and that was me. Taught me how to repair engines of all kinds and there no doubt in my mind he also chosen me to be your sweet heart. Maybe he saw it when we first met at the garage when we first interacted together. You remember when we were testing each other out. I was checking you out and you were diffidently checking me out."

Norman stopped and as he took a drink of his coffee he examined if Bonnie was reacting to his words and sadly he could see no change.

This love, which not only walked with him in dark times, but also shouted with him in good times. He thought, "She at times would get herself in such trouble when she got her mine was set on something. Shoot, she would call me for help hanging on a cliff overhang by her finger nails while clinging to some clip edge."

Norman stood and slowly walked over to Bonnie, bent down and kissed her on the forehead. He looked into her eyes and knew in his heart it was getting to a point he could no longer care for her. He did not have the strength to move her unless she helped and her help was disappearing fast. He kissed her forehead again before returning to his recliner and after he sat, he took a drink of his now cold coffee.

"What am I going to do?" Norman softy said. "I guess I'll call the kids and tell them the bad news."

Norman reached for the phone and thought back when her sickness started. He thought, "I should have known something was wrong when she reported to me it was about to rain and left the windows down on the car. If I remember right it took a week for the seats to dry out."

Norman dialed Clara's number and as it rang he again thought, "I hate having to do this." "Hello," Clara answered.

Norman answered, "This is Dad and I just hate to tell you this. It is time to move your mother into a Nursing Home. I am not able to take care of her by myself anymore."

Clara returned, "Dad, if it is to be? It is to be. I've known this was about to happen last time I visited you and Mom. I hate to hear it for we all know you love her so. I personally think you should have done this long ago."

Norman said, "Maybe I should have. But, I have given your mother the best all my life and the only reason I am doing this I can longer give her my best. I'm just not able. Anyway, I've already establish a room for her at Nub Hill Nursing Home and I'm sure they are expecting us.

I've already given them her medicine records and health history. She'll be in room 23 and she want be alone. She'll have a roommate."

Clara said, "Dad, you want me to come now or later this afternoon. Say around 4est."

Norman answered, "4est be good." "Ok see you then, bye." Clara said.

"Ok," Norman said just before he hung the phone up.

Norman left his recliner and it was not long till he had two bowls of chicken soup setting on the table. He took hold of Bonnie's arm and with a little tolerance he was able to persuade Bonnie to the table where he helped her sit. Tears fill his eyes as he sat down beside her to feed her. This would be the last time he will ever be at home with her sitting across the table from her. The more he taught the more the tears flowed. Here she sat as she has sit so many times in our lives. He could see that she either sat waiting for him to feed her or was she was there because he sat her there. He did not know if she had any feeling for him or not. The blank look she had on her face gave no tells, made up no lies.

"I've lost her and I have no idea when that happened?" Norman said as he wiped the tears from his eyes only to have them explode upon his face again. It took several minutes before Norman was able to feed the soup to her. Each spoon full he had to almost force it into her mouth. He tried encouraging words to no avail.

Norman set the spoon down and with patience led her back to her chair in the living room. Left her and returned to the table to finish his soup. He was so frustrated and hurt. It was taking all his will power to stay calm while asking God to comfort him in his hour of lost.

Slowly the Holy Spirit rose up within his being as he spoke in tongs for almost an hour. As he calmed down his heart was so uplifted from the experience knowing without a doubt everything is going to be alright.

Norman lifted his head toward heaven and said, "Lord, I will morn and I will do it my way. For I am confidence you will bring us together again. Thus as she leaves this house to die, Lord, I am sure you will provide a comfortable death for her. She is the love of my life. The one I woke up in the morning with and the one I went to bed at night with. You have given us three lovely children together and we did our best to make sure they grew up fearing thee. I know Bonnie has put her trust in you as well as me. Both of us have well over the three score and ten you promise us."

As Norman sat lifting his eyes toward the Lord Jesus, he felt a great lifting from off his soul for his sweet Bonnie whom he knew his Lord was about to take home, he humbly said, "Father, if I can I will stay with her at the Nursing Home until she passes away for you know she is the love of my life."

Norman wiped the tears from his eyes and faced toward Bonnie and there in the corner of her eyes he could see tears running down her face. He knew right then that Bonnie was showing him that she understood and would also miss him also. God must have let her hear his prayer.

"Oh God," Norman said as slide out of chair and placed himself upon his knees. He slowly lowered his head into his open hands while all the time crying, "Oh God, Oh God."

Without conscious knowing it Norman began to speak in tongs as the Holy Spirit consume him growing stronger and stronger in him until his tong became God's tongue causing his mouth to tingle when it said, "Masumky malimy camlimy." It was short and he instantly returned to his normal tong for only a minute when the tongs change to English and interpretation of God's word came forth saying, "Worry not and believe says the Lord, as you are one and the same on Earth, the shall be as one and the same in Heaven."

Norman slowly laid himself silently upon the floor still dwelling in the Holy Ghost. His mine going back to God's words and suddenly all worry concerning Bonnie and himself ended right then and there. He lifted himself off the floor and for several minutes could do nothing but shout, "Glory Hallelujah," over and over again.

Eventually, Norman settled down in the Spirit and returned to the living room with a cup of hot coffee and after he checked Bonnie he sat down in the recliner near her. He thought as he sat, "I need to give Bonnie some of her medication and water soon. The Lord sure has reviled himself to me and his love. I made up my mind and with God's help I will never worry about tomorrow again."

Looking toward Bonnie, Norman leaned forward and said, "Bonnie, you can go to heaven anytime now. I'm releasing thee. I'm letting you go. God showed me that I have kept you here mostly for my own greedy reasons. Please accept my humble apologies. It is just that I love you so much I did not want to lose you. God has just shown me I was wrong. I was so wrong. It has now come to the day I was hoping would never happen. I am letting the children place you in a nursing home which I should have done myself. I have arranged everything for your bodily needs here and after you travel home. I will bury you beside your Mother and Dad in our family plot as we have discussed.

You and I have already chosen our casket and best of all everything is paid for leaving the children out of it as we have chosen. Again, I am telling you, I love you and when you leave us, you will be terribly missed."

Norman leaned back in his chair and smile. Reached and took a drink of his now cold coffee. He continued to go over their preparation when his mind wondered over to Brother Leffew at the Church of God. He has been their preacher there going on twenty-four years now and to Norman, he was a very spiritual loving Man of God. Had great knowledge of God's Word and when the Spirit would move in the church he was smart enough to let the Spirit move. He told the church often that the Holy Ghost can do more to minister in five minutes then his preaching could ever do.

Brother Leffew always wore suspenders and Norman laughed when he thought of the time Brother Leffew thought his suspenders were putting a barrier between him and Jesus. Norman thought, "If I remember right it was started because of my loving Bonnie there. I think it was a time he was in one of his doesn't feel holy enough moods. It was Sunday Night service and Brother Leffew been there a little over a year. He had become comfortable with the small congregation of believers in the Church of God and the Holy Ghost had move mightily many times and blessed the church in what he called, "Wet spells. And when the Holy Ghost had not moved mightily in the church for a while he would call them, "Dry Spells." Those words he used then and still does it today. Man, I do love him. I remember it was one of those rainy nights in April making the outside world so gloomy. The service started as it always did with several of the men and women would go into separate rooms to pray. During the prayer time Brother Leffew would always prayed about his message he was to preach that night and that was when I heard him first time say, "Father, I have not felt a visitation of the Holy Ghost for some time now. I feel that there is something I am doing or wearing to cause this."

I looked at him as he continued to pray for his message tonight and as he again asked for a mighty movement of the

Holy Ghost. I quickly joined him in his prayer as I lifted upped my hands toward Heaven asking the same question to God. I was joined by the other men in the room.

Slowly the Holy Ghost enveloped us, till we were all speaking in tongs. If it wasn't for the music and singing outside in the church, I believed we would all just sat in that room and dwell in the Spirit for a while. Brother Leffew stood and said, "Come on fellows. It's show time,"

I laugh at his statement and more I thought upon it I realized he spoke the truth. Silently to myself I said, "I guess it is show time for you and every preacher in this country, the moment they stand before their congregation."

I took my usual seat on the front row allowing me the freedom to worship my Lord and Savior in the Spirit. Bonnie always sat with her sister Judy in the seats just back of me and as the singing began, I reach out toward God through the Spirit but when the music stopped it appeared the Spirit movement did also.

Brother Leffew after several songs said, "Folks, I have been yearning for a movement of the Holy Ghost and I feel in some way it is my fault he has not move for us. Sister Bonnie has suggested it was my suspensors so before God and the congregation I'm taking them off. We laugh as he slowly unhooked one side then the other and there before us was Brother Leffew stood suspensor less. Without them, he seemed shorter in his light yellow shirt.

Brother Leffew motion for the singers to continue and

after a moment they began to sing, "I shall not be moved." He turned and began to shout as suddenly the Spirit hit him and slowly the whole congregation join him as if Jesus had just walked down the aisle and took a seat in front.

Norman thought, "Over the last few years I've taken Bonnie before the Lord several times for a healing until I realized by the Spirit there is no easy way to die."

Ten
CHAPTER

Norman watched from the porch as Clara tried to place Bonnie into the backseat of her SUV. She appeared very upset and he could just make out she had teary eyes. As he watched Clara, he thought how lovely she looked. In fact both girls had kept their bodies healthy even after the children left home. Still there was one thing both Clara and Kota always did was they wore their hair different and still do.

Clara always likes to wear her hair short while Kota always wore it long to give herself a sexy appearance. If not they would look like twins and he always figured that was why they wore their hair different, to look different. I don't why, for they were not alike at all.

And there was Clara trying to get Bonnie to move farther into the car so she could shut the door. There was no response accept Bonnie did look at her and smiled. It only made the scene sadder as she had to carefully push her Mother into the Car which dried her eyes. Then as she closed the car door said, "I hope she comes out better then she went in."

Norman could do nothing but laughed at Clara's frustration. Watching the scene from the porch Norman thought it was quite funny.

Clara looked at him and the tension she had gotten himself into drifted right into laughter for she realized it was kind of funny. When she looked back at her Mother, tears came into her eyes as she said, "Darn Mom, why did you have to get sick?"

Norman upon hearing Clara's word said, "Clara, there is no easy way to die. God has chosen it for us and having done so will always remind us to walk the straight and narrow in Heaven."

"Oh, Dad," Clara spoke back with a frustrated sound in her voice.

"Well it is true," Norman said as he walked around to the other side of the car, opened the door and took a seat on the other side of Bonnie who just looked upon him and gave her usually smile she been given everybody sense she started it a few months earlier as she heath slowly became such it had gone beyond his ability to care for her. Norman just smile back to the love of his life. Norman smile even grew deeper as he reminded himself, "She sure made a home not only for him and their children also. I know and concluded a long time ago our home was often times more for them than me."

But as he watched the girls gather themselves into the front seats, Norman thought as they settled in for the ride, "It was the way God wanted it to be. I guess. In fact, there is not a creature in or on the Earth that does not care for its young. What makes man any different?"

Clara from behind the steering wheel, reached back and tapped Norman on the knee and said, "You ready for this, Daddy?"

Norman tilted his head as he always did when one of the children asked a question he was not ready to answer but instead asked, "You have placed our cloths in her room and the few essentials we will need?"

"Yes Daddy." Kota answered not turning to looking back. Afraid she would just burst into tears if she did. Bonnie was her mother and to see her as she had become was very hard for her to handle. She thought as she glanced at her sister, "I am sure glad Clara strong enough to handle this. I had to force myself to come today and right now I wish I was back at the house."

After they had backed out onto the road, Clara beside her said, "You ok Kota?"

"Not really," she answered. "I was just thinking about Mom when we were little young girls."

Clara placed the car in forward and as she left the house she said,

"I know one thing. When we were children we could not get away with anything. Mom seem to always know what we were going to do before we even thought of it and she would always would say, "Remember girls, I was a young girl too.""

Clara's words broke the tension Kota had been feeling and she laughed as she turned her head toward Norman after she had examining her Mother and said, "I should have given you two a lot more support than I did, Dad. But I always felt you didn't want mine or Clara's help. In fact, Daddy, I can count on one hand the number of times you have called us for our help and that was usually to drive you and Mom to the doctor or to some Tent Revival."

Norman just shook his head, "Yes," as he said, "Our door was always open and you could have walked in and sat awhile anytime day or night."

Kota turned and faced back down the road and said, "We did when we were a lot younger, Daddy. But remember, we are not young anymore and we have grandchildren to prove it."

"I guess you do at that." Norman answered as he took hold of Bonnie's hand beside him.

Norman listened to the chatter of the girls as he watched them drive through the Gafftop housing area and the few stores that were still in business there.

Norman thought, "In all the years he has live here, the town never grew any bigger then what it was when I was a child. The only real change has been the oil rigs pumping around that not been there but for the most part the town of Gafftop has never change and that includes the rice fields located around it."

There was only one building gone Norman wished was still around and that was the old high school gym where Bonnie and he would go dancing twice a month. The children learned to dance there and many a girl and boy became girlfriend and boyfriend at the dances. But when they consolidated the schools and close the school down, the Gym had been torn down also. It was told it had become too dangerous of a building to have activities in. But he always taught it was to make sure the school was not open back up again. What better way to prevent that from happening then to level it to the ground?

Normal smile as he thought, "But I guess the biggest blessing for the Town of Gafftop, it has never had a direct hit by any Gulf Hurricane. The water got up but really never flooded the town. The only word he could think of for that was Lucky.

Norman left the view of the rice field and glance over at the love of his life basically asleep with her eyes wide open. She had been the best thing that has ever entered his life and supported him in so many ways throughout their marriage. Thinking back to that Gym and the dances she sure was a great dancer and everyone that ever dance with her said the same thing.

"I guess learning to dance was a gift from Mom and Dad." Norman thought. "They loved to dance and away we went to the gym when I was a boy. I learn all the dance steps and I think I invented a few steps for myself. I guess the other gift was music but for some reason I never did joined the school band. I guess I wanted it to be part of my life and not my whole life I guess."

Then Norman smiled as he thought back to his guitar in the trunk of the car. He loved to play it and the Gospel Songs that were his favorite and over the last twenty years the only music he would play. He always like it when Bonnie song with him specially the song, "I want have to worry anymore."

Then under his breath he sung, "Down here the load gets heavy and the road is rough and long. Sometimes my feet get so weary and oh so tired…....."

Glancing over at Bonnie he felt the tears that came into his eyes.

"Darn you Bonnie." He thought.

Norman glanced down at his legs to force his eyes off her and thought, "She was a pistol alright. Stood by the children if they were right and if they were wrong, watch out. Even I would run."

Lifted his eyes upward and looked upon his two girls. Thinking of getting his mind off Bonnie sitting beside him, he looked upon the girls and thought back to the girl's childhood and how they were so different. You would never think as they sat in front of them how wild and different they were. I was sure glad they out grew some of it. I'm still not sure of Kota thou. She was the wild one. Dress the part also. Bonnie did not fight with her over her cloths choices and even when Koto seem to be at her worst, Bonnie would twist her thinking in a way that I could not touch or want to.

I guess Kota was my favorite between the two girls. She always expressed herself freely and Bonnie always kept their girl stuff between them girls alone and in fact, I did not even want to know.

Now Clara on the other hand was conserved and always made good grades in school. Not that she was perfect by any means. Being smart and always wanting her way she was. But surprising she did not dress the part. Wore what the other girls wore and hair style. I sometimes thought we should have called her laughter, for when she was little she laughed at everything and everybody.

While on the other hand Kota being older was not but she did like to be the center of attention and wanted to sing. She would get before us and with a play mike in her hand, sing one of the songs off the radio she had memorized while twisting her body this way and that. I told Bonnie that I thought her dancing was to reviling and all she said was, "Leave us girls alone."

I would leave them always thinking, "Mom knows best for after all they are girls and I cannot think or act as they do and I have no idea most of the time, what they are thinking."

Kota broke my wondering thinking as she twisted around in her seat and said, "Daddy, do you remember when you and Mom made Gumbo?"

"I sure do and it sure was good wasn't it?" I answered wondering where her question was leading too.

Still twisted she answered, "It sure was. I was wondering do you still have some you put in quart jars somewhere."

"There still a few in the closet." I answered. "I have not thought of making Gumbo in a long time. Did you know your mother actually learn how to make in from my mother, your Grandma?"

Kota looked at her mother a second who was just staring out the window and asked, "Do you still have the recipe for it somewhere. Clara and I are thinking of entering the Gumbo Contest over at Alta Loma this summer. We are almost sure Mom's Gumbo would win and the Grand Prized is a nice fishing rig."

Her reason was a little funny to me as I smile at her and said, "I know that contest and a few jars of gumbo want do you. You will have to set up a cooking system and use our all aluminum four-gallon pot to make the gumbo right there before the judges and I know two of them go to our church."

Before Kota could answered me, Clara said, "We were thinking you might have enough stored upped somewhere so we would not have to cook. Just pour it in the pot and heat."

There was a pause as she finished. Then almost as one we broke out with laughter as the concept became quite funny.

As they settle down and returned to her forward position Kota said, "Mother sure knew how to cook."

I a little more power in my voice I said, "You were not really eating at your Mother's cooking."

Clara maintaining her eye sight on the road ahead said, "That was Mother's cooking. I've watched her make many of a supper and holiday meals. Just what do you mean not her cooking?" Kota turned and looked at her Dad and said, "Yea."

"Don't get me wrong, girls," I answered. "Your Mother was a good cook and all those wonderful Cajon Dishes, well, they came straight from Grandma. I mean every last one of them."

Kota said, "You are joking right?"

I shook my head no as I said, "After a few months of marriage I soon realized your Mother could not cook. The times she smoked up the house and over cooked the food. She was trying and one day your Grandma stopped by and I explained the problem to her. The next thing I knew, here came your Grandma with cookbook in hand.

Soon I was coming home from work to see some of the best Cajon dishes sitting on table waiting for me and far awhile I was eating like the King on the Hill. I really guess it never stopped eaten them. Once your Grandma figured she had taught your Mother she only came by now and then to check out one of her favorites Mother was cooking. I know one thing she never again did she burn a pan and as you know, the food was cook always cook to perfection."

As I finish, Clara said, "Mom could handle spices, alright and she must have learned from Grandma, for I remember many a dish that Grandma made was just likes Mothers. Maybe I should say, "Mother's Cajon Dishes were just like Grandma's?"

Clara and Kota continued to discuss the different between Grandma's cooking and Bonnie's. I chose not to get involved and just glace over at the love of my life. She been dead a long time but her body just does not know it. But I tapped her leg and said, "Bonnie I believe right after we were married, when we had no children I believe was most wonderful time in my life for your fine cooking. I remember I guess it right after Mother started coming over and teaching you and I would come home and there on the table was a Cajon Shrimp dish and as I took my first spoon full I quickly notice there was something missing. I never said anything but my facial gave me away as I hesitated for my second bite."

"You don't like it do you?" Bonnie said. "I made it

just like your Mother showed me and there seems to be something missing are I put something in that was not to be used."

"It is not that bad," I said supportively but Bonnie answered, "Yes it is,"

I did not answer as Bonnie began to pace the floor with her thinking cap on before me. I knew I better not interrupt her and after a bit I meekly said, "It appeared as if there was no seasoning in the sauce."

"Seasoning?" she returned. It was as if a light went off in her head as she looked at me and said, "I forgot the Roux, Row and whatever it's called."

Having the door open to her heart, I took advantage of it and asked, "How it going between Mother and you anyway?"

"She is bound and determined to make me a Cajon cook is what she doing." She answered with a huff and a puff. "But I do have to admit, she is good a good cook but is not a good teacher. Sometimes I can't make heads or tails on how to make one of her good Cajon Dishes. The way she details, how I do this are that gets lost as I try to grasp just what she is covering. Here just Look?" Bonnie and handed me a note book.

As I open it, Bonnie kept pointed into it and said, "Look at those notes. I wrote down her exact words and I cannot make sense of them."

Sure enough, the way Bonnie wrote down Mom's words

I could see why. Most sentences were half done and Spices were mention with no measurements. As examined one of the recipes, I suddenly remembered Mother does not use measuring spoons. It was a pence of this a pence that and a tablespoon was in the palm of your hand.

"Bonnie," I said, "I can see Mother did not teach you how she measured spices?"

"Yes she did," she answered, "I just can't get the hang of it and always afraid I put way too much spice into the recipe. I wish she would use measure spoons and did you know she said that these Cajon Recipes she been given me so far has been handed down from Mother to Daughter over several generations. I just don't want to mess up and it seems all I do is just that."

Bonnie turned and took a seat at the kitchen table. Then as I set the note book on the table I took a seat beside her and said, "Honey, Sweetie Pie, Sugar Plum, I never told you this for I was taught to cook by her and my Grandma. I became the sauce maker. I can teach you how to make a Roux."

"You teach me?" she answered, "Shoot I beat you can't even spell it."

"No, really she did," I answered her back as I stood and calmly walked over to the gas stove and took hold of the large cast iron skillet before turning to her and saying, "I can too spell it, R-o-u-x."

"Oh, so that how you spell it." Bonnie said just before

William Gaillard Ellis Jr

she burst out into laughter. I could not help myself and quickly join in and just when I was about to settled down Bonnie said, "And she said I have ten more sauces to learn."

Her words brought another round of laughter as her meaning for her words became clear. I just shook my head clearing it as I turned the gas on and place the skillet upon it and said, "Come here and I'll show you for it is really very simple."

Bonnie stood and as I moved out of the way, took a stand before the stove and she calmly said, "I'm waiting."

"First thing in making a Roux or any of Mother's sauces we must fetch what you are going to put in it first." I answered began reaching for placing on the counter top the oil, two cups of water, the flour, oregano, thyme, garlic power, bay leaves, one small opened can of tomato sauce and last I took the chopped onions out of the freezer I knew would be there. Then looking at her, I placed the powered cayenne pepper on the counter wonder should I use it or not.

I left the counter top to fetch the Red Wine and said, "I gathered all the ingredients and as you see there not much. It really was quite simple. If you are ready we will start, we will start with the spices."

As I took a coffee cup from the cupboard and place it by the spices, I said, "A pence for Mother, is a quarter teaspoon. But two big pence's is a teaspoon and if Mother thinks she need more she'll pence it. I for one use measuring spoons

162

and I always put all my spices in a cup. I know Mother don't for she'll add the spices later then I do. I found added them early seems to me enhance the spice flavor of the Roux."

Bonnie suddenly pushed me out of the way and as she took hold to the Thyme bottle said, "I'll do it."

Ignoring me she looked at her notes and thinking out loud as she placed the spices into the cup said, "A pence is a quarter teaspoon so I put a quarter teaspoon of it into the cup, a tablespoon of Oregano, a heaping tablespoon of garlic, salt, and two bay leaves."

Bonnie turned back to the stove and placed the skillet back upon the burner and as she reached for the oil said, "I do remember I am first to place some oil in the skillet. But I do not know how much. Your Mother just pores some in."

I just smiled as I handed her a tablespoon and said, "Its two over flowing tablespoons is what she starts with and the oil is heated to where it just starts to smoke, add two tablespoons of flour and whisked it letting the flour turn red, Mother like it real dark red. Add the onions and whisked them around, add the spices when you think onions is cook enough and whisk the spices mixing then just before you add the tomato sauce, whisked it two tablespoon of the red wine and when everything seems right add the two cups of water, bring it to a boil and let it simmer."

Bonnie followed my directions and soon had a simmering red sauce before her and smiled as she turned and said,

"That was easier than I thought and now I know how to read the way your Mother measures spices."

"Did she tell you how to thicken sauces?" I asked being and acting as if I knew something she didn't.

"You think you are smart, don't ya," Bonnie returned. "But your Mother did and that was to place two tablespoons of butter and one tablespoon of flour in a bowl and mixed them real good before adding the mixture to the sauce."

She took a step forward and smiling placed her arms around my neck and pulled herself close to me making sure her tits were pushed against my chess and as I placed my arms around her, she said, "See I did know and I think with your Mother's help, I will become the best cook in this house, your Mother's house and in fact the whole town of Gafftop."

"I think you will be at that," I said as I bent and we kissed. One of those tongue to tongue kisses and I've learned she does like to move that tong of hers into my mouth and of course I returned the favor.

She removed her left hand form my neck and moved it between us and felt of my penis that had not yet become hard as it always does when Bonnie becomes fresh with me. My mind was still centered on our kissing but her fondling me broke our kissing and I could see her eyes were close as she felt of me.

She wanted love and I smiled as I look upon her head bent still in a kissing position. I gave her a quick kiss and took her hand from off my neck saying, "You keep that up I'm going be changing underwear."

Bonnie open her eyes and looked me in the face and a smile grew upon it as she said, "I was just talking with it is all. How did he fill and seems he said, "Ready to go." Then I asked him has Norman been chasing and running around and know what he said? He said Norman only has one love."

She gave another squeeze to my penis but as she pulled away put her hand under by balls and slowly pulled upward. I wasn't sorry she left my now pulsing penis at all. It was full of that special feeling I get within that feels so good it can become quite over powering. I love it as Bonnie would bring the feeling upwards from within me till I explode in pleasure that can become so intense I would only morn and then the end of my penis becomes so sensitive that if Bonnie rubbed it I would want to stop her.

Bonnie turned back to the Roux and said, "William, I want a baby."

I did not answer her I adjusting my harden penis in my pants when her words hit me, "I looked up from off my groin area and took a position behind her while placing both my arms across her and said, "A baby would be nice but does that depends if your horny enough."

As Bonnie stirred the sauce she said, "I been thinking just how I was going to love you tonight all day. That is why I left you alone the last two days for I wanted this

Friday night be a special night. I just know when we are done tonight and you go to sleep that in nine month I will give birth to a healthy baby girl."

"What if it's a boy?" I asked.

Bonnie kind of laughed as she said, "I'll have the doctor put it back and tell God to give me another and it better be a girl."

I let go of her and as I handed her the Cajon Dish from the table and said, "Remember a Roux is really a seasoning and you only add what you think the Cajon Dish needed. It other words Bonnie you put a small amount at a time until you have gotten the favor acquired for the Cajon Dish you were fixing at the time. I was never allowed to do that, I assure you for Mother and Grandma would say, "What we add is our little secret." But I knew what they did. Just add a little bit of the Roux until you have the favor you want. Sometime she would have one non pepper roux and two are three hot pepper roux's and mix the Cajon dish to how hot she wanted to make it and Grandpa like his hot. I remember at one family reunion there was about fifteen different Cajon dishes and everyone brought their own Roux's. I mean there must have been at lease twenty different types and around them when located their names. Then you would add whatever you thought to be the best favor for that Cajon Dish and put a dash of the Roux into it. Daddy like Aunt Bee's for she made the hottest of the all the hot Roux's. As for me, I would only get Mothers or Grandma's for I knew they were not hot. But I outgrew that and was soon putting the same Roux Grandpa used on my Cajon plate of food and I've must admit that Aunt Bee's Roux was by far the best tasting and Mother or Grandma never got her to tell them her secret."

"Never," Bonnie asked as she adjusted the flame for the Cajon dish to heat.

"I tell you what," I said as I left her to take a seat at the table. "Why don't we go visit Aunt Bee this weekend and see if she would give you her Hot Roux recipe if you promise not to give it to Mother or Grandma."

Bonnie turned the burners off and taking hold of the Cajon Dish added two spoons full of the Roux to it. Tasted it just she before adding two more spoon full of Roux and smile as she turned from the stove saying, "Now this is a true Cajon Dish if I ever tasted one." She seems quite happy as she set the pot upon the table, reached and grabbed two bowls and spoons from the cabinets, set them beside the slightly steaming Cajon Dish. Then taken hold of a smaller bowl she placed some of the roux in it and added pence are two of the red pepper, stirred and set it also beside the Cajon Dish and upon seeing the smile she gave me, I always felt when Bonnie smile at me with that sparkle in her eye it was a, "*I love you* kind of smile."

We sat at that table admiring the great taste her Cajon dish had become and I assure my mouth was on fire. I did not tell her a dash of red pepper would have been the right amount. I guess will come later when Mother or Grandma will tell her the secrets of handling pepper.

I just knew enough about pepper to give a dish I had cooked for myself all the heat I desired at the time.

My mind wondered around as we sat eating with her admiring me and me admiring her. When suddenly I felt her foot side up my leg and could not help it as I lowered my butt forward letting her foot wonder around over the groin area and of course knew I was getting a hard on which in some ways I did not want to happen but her toes kept pushing on it and it felt good as that special feeling that sometimes was so good that at times I would morn. I remember a Professor on TV describe it as a pain. It may be a pain but I liked it and when she left my groin area my desire was for her to stay.

"Darn Bonnie, you done got him up again." I laughed as I readjusted my hard dick in my pants.

"He felt real good to me," Bonnie returned as she stood, walked around the table and placed her head on my shoulder and arms across my back and her other hand began rubbing my chest.

Then in a sexy sounding voice she said, "Now my big good-looking hunk of a man would I ever side my hand down like this to fine what I'm looking for." Slowly her hand worked down my belly and slowly she moved down across my hard penis and across my balls.

By now I lost all control of myself and just sat there

enjoying her fondling me. Then slowly she came back up across my penis, up my belly and up to my face and said, "Now would I ever do such a thing and feel that pretty thing you got and get you weak where you can't move. I got you where I want you completely under my control."

I glance sideways at her and smile as I said, "I'm helpless as a baby lamb that is for sure."

She looked into my eyes and smiled as she said, "I guess it is alright for me to do this," She then bent over with her eyes looking into mine and only left them as she reached down and we kissed. Not a quick kiss either. It was one of those tongue fighting kisses with each trying to stick their tongue into the others mouth. Of course she won and while we were kissing I ran my hand up her leg and found no panties and rub the hair above her pussy for a second before running my fingers over the skin covering of her pussy. She gave a morn as she took her lips away from mine, sticking her chest out and with head up and eyes closed dwell upon the feeling I gave her while rubbing her pussy and only stopped as I felt her wetness.

She opens her eyes and looked into mind saying, "I think it is time for a shower. Don't you?"

I smiled and dwell on what was going to happen in the shower a second before answering her with, "You going to undress me before are after the shower?"

Bonnie left me and very sexy like, said, "Big boy, you just follow me and fine out."

She continued to walk backwards as I stood and her finger motioning and her saying, "Come on, Come on."

It was kind of funny and I actually laugh at her attics as I follow her into the bathroom. After I entered she calmly closed the door and smile saying, "That just in case you want to run."

Standing beside the sink I answered, "Now why would I want do that when I'm about to be washed like a baby."

"Oh be quiet and let me enjoy this," she said as she turned me to face her and began unbuttoning my shirt. She pulled the shirt tail out and with my help removed my shirt from off me and let it fall to the floor as she ran her hand across my chest looking into my eyes watching her as she rub downwards upon my very hard penis. She then set herself upon her knees and gently removed my shoes and socks before she reached and undid my belt buckle and gently lowered the zipper.

Then looking up into my face Bonnie smiled as she undid my pants button and pulling them down off my butt exposing my groin area bulging out of my white underwear. Then having me pick a leg up at a time removed my jeans from me and toss them into a corner as she slowly pulled my underwear down removing them as she did the pants.

But she did not stand as she examined my groin area carefully while feeling my balls and running her hand up and down my penis feeling its shape. Then reached and kissed it before letting it slid into her mouth feeling the shape of it with her tongue for a second. Kissed it again and I help her stand.

She did not have to tell me as I gently pull lifted her nightgown over her head exposing her fine firm tits. I tossed it in the corner with my pants. Felt of both her tits with the ends semi hard before lowering myself and removing her slippers. Before standing I did a quick kiss upon the hairs above her groin and taught of doing more when Bonnie took my head and said, "Not now,"

I stood facing her naked body she left me saying, "While I'm getting the water ready why don't you shave and brush your teeth. And I'll be waiting in the shower. As quick as I could've shaved and brushed my teeth, which allow my harden penis to relax a little. When I was done I entered the shower and Bonnie push me under the flowing water and began to wash me starting around my feet and working upward.

Turning me when needed and left my groin area till last before just gently washed it feeling of my balls and pushing upward a little with them. I tried to touch her and she pushed my hand away saying, "Not yet, I'm not done with you."

She turned my face into the water and washed my back and even down the crack in my butt. As she was doing that I thought, "I wonder why they call it a Crack, Butt Crack?"

I was enjoying her wondering hands when they left me and Bonnie said, "Your turn."

I made sure my face and back was clear of any soap before I removed myself from the shower water and let Bonnie take my place. There was smile on her face as she took hold of my hand that held the washrag and brought slowly to her tits and calmly let go of my hand and she ran her hand under my balls and lightly squeezed. I slowly brought my free hand down to her groin and with the shower water flowing over our heads we kissed.

We just stood together letting the shower water run across our heads and down our bodies dwelling in the moment of being together more at being as one, then at any time in our lives. The moment we separated my heart exploded with a love for Bonnie that went way beyond our physical bodies. All I could do was to stare into her face with the shower water running across it with her eyes closed. I move my hand upward and across her flat belly and felt of her belly button.

Suddenly she pushed me away from her and I could see her face had this unique seducing image about it. In fact, Bonnie's face was just plain sexy and as she opens her eyes and viewed me, very gently said, "Let us go to bed."

I stayed in the shower and watched Bonnie dry herself off starting with the hair. As she dried her hair, her very nice shapely body and as she dried herself her tits one could say, "They wiggled and at times, they bounced."

I caught the towel she threw at me and left the bathroom still drying herself off. As I took the towel and began to dry myself, I looked down at my now calmed down penis and said, "I hope you can handle what she is after. Just hang in there," I laughed knowing the darn thing would always explode when I don't want it too.

As I finish drying my hair with the hair dryer, I could hear Bonnie in the bed room drying hers. So I tied a towel around me and waited till she was done to enter the bed room tuning out the light. As I caught a glanced at the bed and noticed the bed cover was gone and only bed sheets remain. Bonnie sat on the bed with only one of her pajama tops opened around her allowing her tits to be seen but not seen. There were two glasses in her hands full of red wine I like to use if I cooked. She held one out to me and as I took it I let the towel drop away and stood looking down on her letting my penis just stand and look at her.

Bonnie reached and rubbed it and its glow increase in me. Then as she pulled her hand away, held the glass up before me and said, "Let us thank God that the baby will be healthy and a girl."

I tapped my glass to hers in agreement and we both drank the wine together. As she finished, I took her glass, turned out the lights and began to crawl into the bed not really knowing what Bonnie was going to do. My groin was now a solid glow.

"Lay on your belly and be quiet, Please," she ordered in her somewhat sexy voice which sounded quit enticing as

I she felt of my glowing groin area just before I stretched out upon the bed.

As I settled with my hands under my head I felt her begin to massage my feet feeling their shape. Slowly she worked up both my legs and onto my butt where she stayed awhile running from one side to the other before moving up my back gently working her fingers deep into my back muscles.

By now I had closed my eyes liking the feel of her wonderful hands and loving the sensation her hands gave me moving down to my behind where she stayed even reaching deep between my legs and lightly felt of by balls. My grown area continued to pulse with each touch of her hands and even continued as she moved down my legs. But when she reached my feet she said, "Please turn over."

I did not open my eyes as I turned and even kept them closed as she move her hands upward and around my pulsing groin and up upon my chest. There they stopped and I felt her leg crossing my body and felt her pussy as my penis entered her and the warmth and wetness within her. Slowly she moved herself up and down and I was thankful for her making me eat a lot of chocolate which always cause me to delay my organism. I lay motionless as she worked herself up and down enjoying the feel of her movement upon me and every now and then pushed upward to meet her downward truss.

As my groin glow increase and increase, I reach and

began calmly massaging her tits. The image of my penis in her magnified my groin glow till it exploded forth as the organism consumes me. The sensation at the end of my penis as Bonnie moved, was almost too overbearing. I wanted to scream but instead just moaned. As I became quiet, I suddenly felt Bonnie stiffen in her own organism and her reaction was to pump her body harder on my penis.

Eventually Bonnie settled down and lowered her head down upon my chess placing her arms on each side of me. I placed my hands across her back and held her feeling the great love she had for me. At that moment in time, I knew I was going to take care of her the rest of our lives. I knew we were to have several children. That she will carry my name in her and with her everywhere she goes and did it as my wife, my friend, my lover and always carried herself as the Mother of our children. Strict when needed and I know she will become to me and the children the best cook in whole City of Gafftop able to fry fish and shrimp and make the best Gumbo for sure. With the children, she will rejoice when they did well in school and never afraid to get right down and dirty with them during their teen years. But mostly she will always be my friend, my lover and now, my Bonnie, my precious Bonnie, sitting beside me in this car can only hold my hand which I guess we have always done. Like every time she and I walked into church to worship our Savior and when she gave birth to our three children. We held hands every night before we drifted off to sleep and if I could have counted the kisses, I guess they would have been in the millions, my Bonnie, my love, I guess my aching heart is trying to say, "Good bye my love."

Norman could not help it as tears filled his eyes.

Dear reader, "I hope the words I wrote justified this novel in being called, "A Love Story."